Sou
Cruis

BOOK 21

Hope Callaghan

hopecallaghan.com
Copyright © 2021
All rights reserved.

This book is a work of fiction. Although places mentioned may be real, the characters, names and incidents, and all other details are products of the author's imagination and are fictitious. Any resemblance to actual organizations, events, or actual persons, living or dead is purely coincidental.

No part of this publication may be copied, reproduced in any format, by any means, electronic or otherwise, without prior consent from the copyright owner and publisher of this book.

Visit my website for new releases and special offers:
hopecallaghan.com

CONTENTS

Cast of Characters

Mildred "Millie" Sanders-Armati. Millie, heartbroken after her husband left her for one of his clients, decides to take a position as assistant cruise director aboard the mega cruise ship, Siren of the Seas. From day one, she discovers she has a knack for solving mysteries, which is a good thing since some sort of crime is always being committed on the high seas.

Recently married to the ship's captain, Millie has embarked on a new adventure on board Siren of the Seas.

Annette Delacroix. Director of Food and Beverage on board Siren of the Seas, Annette has a secret past and is the perfect accomplice in Millie's investigations. Annette is the "Jill of all Trades" and isn't afraid to roll up her sleeves and help out a friend in need.

Catherine "Cat" Wellington. Cat is the most cautious of the group of friends and prefers to help Millie from the sidelines, but when push comes to shove, Millie can count on Cat to risk life and limb in the pursuit of justice.

Danielle Kneldon. Danielle first found her way on board Siren of the Seas working undercover. After her assignment ended, she snagged a position on board the ship and joined Millie and the gang to round out their "Super Sleuths" to a team of four.

"For you were once darkness, but now you are light in the Lord. Live as children of light." Ephesians 5:8 NI

Chapter 1

"If you move a bit more toward the middle, I'll be able to get a great deal of Stonehenge in and a fantastic shot of the clear skies, a blessing for us these days," their guide drawled in his utterly charming British accent.

Millie, Annette, Cat and Danielle squeezed in even closer, with the UNESCO World Heritage Site directly behind them.

"Perfect. Lovely." He finished taking the photo and handed Annette her cell phone. "Is there anywhere else round Salisbury you would care to visit?"

"I think I've seen enough, and my feet are getting sore." Annette's eyes swept across the vista. "It is a sight to behold, but I'm ready to go home."

"Me too." Millie was equally excited yet sad that Siren of the Seas' summer season in the British Isles had come to an end.

The last group of cruise passengers had disembarked that morning. Within hours, the ship and crew would welcome a new set of passengers, those embarking on the thirteen-day voyage across the Atlantic to the Port of Miami.

It had been a wonderful summer, full of amazing sights and adventures, memories Millie would treasure forever. But she was eagerly looking forward to new adventures in the "ABC Islands," islands she'd never visited before.

"It's been an eventful summer," Cat said. "A lot has happened."

"Including a new beau for Cat," Danielle teased.

"Now that you mention it," Cat smiled, "Andy's planned a surprise excursion for us this afternoon. He told me to wear sneakers, pack a pair of flip-flops, a windbreaker and an umbrella."

"So, expect a little of everything," Millie teased. "Sun, rain and wind."

"I have a hunch he's taking me to a museum and then out for a late lunch to sample some authentic Scottish or British dishes."

"If it's Scottish...a word of warning," Danielle said. "Skip the haggis."

"I've heard of haggis but can't remember much about it," Millie said. "What is it?"

"Disgusting," Annette chuckled. "Unless you're Scottish, of course. It's sheep guts ground into sausage."

Cat's eyes widened in horror. "Seriously? I won't eat that. Is there anything else I should avoid?"

"I shouldn't have said anything."

"I tried Cullen skink. It's fish soup," Millie said. "Speaking of fish, you can't go wrong with fish and chips."

"Fish and chips sounds safe. I think I'll stick to something I know."

"Millie and I are hosting a small bon voyage party in the galley." Annette explained that they had invited Halbert Pennyman, the homeless man who lived in a warehouse a stone's throw from the dock, along with the security guards he had befriended over the summer months, to join them for a goodbye luncheon in the ship's galley.

During the luncheon, they planned to surprise Halbert with a few parting gifts.

"I'm going to miss Halbert." Millie could feel her throat clog at the thought of saying goodbye to her friend, certain that today would be the last day she would ever see him again.

"It will be a little sad." Annette slipped her arm through Millie's arm. "And on that note, it's time for us to head back."

Roland, their tour guide, began leading them back to the main path.

"You went on a lot of excursions, Millie. Which was your favorite?" Cat asked.

"It's hard to pick just one. I loved visiting Blarney Castle with Amit. Loch Ness is high on the list. The countryside was amazing."

"I figured you would say Skara Brae," Annette joked.

Cat made a choking sound. "Don't remind us."

"Skara Brae, by far, was the most memorable. Being trapped in a haunted house and having Siren of the Seas leave us behind is something I'll never forget."

"Thank God Nic rescued us," Cat said. "We would probably still be there."

Millie grew quiet as she thought about all the wonderful British Isles' ports, the excursions, not to mention the adventures. "I'm sure Sharky will never forget Southampton."

"Where he was kidnapped and held for ransom." Annette veered off the path to avoid a large rock. "I bet he'll never fib and tell a woman he's captain of a cruise ship again."

"Now that you mention Sharky, I wonder what his surprise is." For days now, the ship's maintenance supervisor had been anxiously awaiting their return to Southampton. He'd spent countless hours with Donovan, going over what he claimed was a valuable tool for not only maintenance, but also for the ship's security and safety department.

"Donovan stopped by the gift shop last night and made a comment that Sharky was driving him nuts," Cat said.

"I can't wait to find out what it is." Millie turned her attention to Annette. "So, what about you,

Annette? What was your favorite port or excursion here in the British Isles?"

"That's a no-brainer...this! I've had fun exploring this pile of rocks and, of course, spending time with my friends."

Millie had to agree. It was a fitting last day, to be outside enjoying the fresh air, considering they would be stuck on board the ship for several long days with no land in sight. It had been a picture-perfect day spent with her besties.

During the ride back to the port, Roland pointed out several landmarks and areas of interest.

Millie took it all in, briefly wondering if she would ever visit again. She and Nic had tried to plan a trip to Bertoli, the small Italian fishing village where he'd been born and raised, but it hadn't worked out and the couple decided that, during their next break, they would travel to Michigan to visit Millie's family. From there they would fly to Italy, splitting their break between both of their families.

As they drew closer to the port, Millie spied the smokestacks of another cruise ship docked nearby.

"I wonder if we'll be back again next year." Cat echoed Millie's thoughts.

"Nic doesn't seem to think so. I heard Alaska is being considered for our next summer season."

"Alaska? Are you serious?" Danielle playfully punched Millie in the arm. "Is there something you're not telling us?"

"It's only talk right now, so don't get your hopes up. Alaska is one that's being discussed although a decision will have to be made soon. From what little my tight-lipped husband is sharing, we'll for sure be based out of the World Cruise Center."

"Where's that?" Cat asked.

"Los Angeles," Millie and Annette said in unison.

"LA?" Cat wrinkled her nose. "Yuck."

Annette pursed her lips. "Why is it yuck? LA gives us several options. Mexico, Hawaii, and Alaska."

Danielle clapped her hands. "We could do the whole *Love Boat* itinerary."

"Puerto Vallarta and Acapulco," Millie said. "I love to watch the re-runs when I have time."

"You should write a book," Annette said. "Since you're such a snoop, you could call it *Murder She Wrote Meets the Love Boat*. We could pitch it to some literary agents and try to get it turned into a television show."

Cat laughed. "Millie has had enough adventures to release a whole series. She would be famous."

"Ha. Ha. Very funny." Millie changed the subject. "I think any of those sounds like fun...Mexico to follow in the footsteps of the television series. Hawaii or Alaska because they sound amazing."

"If you have any pull at all, I'm rooting for Hawaii," Cat said.

"My vote is Mexico," Danielle said.

"Put me down for Alaska," Annette chimed in.

Cat tapped the window with her fingernail, pointing to Siren of the Seas' smokestack rising majestically off in the distance. "We're almost home. I see our ship."

The friends grew quiet as their van rounded the bend, passing by the National Oceanography Centre. On the opposite side of the street was Queen's Park, a small, picturesque park Millie and Scout had visited many times.

"Uh-oh." Annette craned her neck. "Something's going on over at the park."

"You're kidding." Millie's heart sank at the number of patrol vehicles across the street from the port...mere steps from Halbert's home.

Chapter 2

Millie scrambled out of the van as soon as it stopped, hastily thanking Roland for the private tour and rewarding him with a generous tip before making a beeline for the Queen's Park entrance.

She, along with the others, edged past a group of onlookers, including several of the ship's crewmembers, circling around until they reached an empty spot near a cluster of uniformed officers. Millie let out a sigh of relief when she spotted Halbert standing between two of them.

The ship's head of security, Dave Patterson, was also there.

"Can you see anything?" Danielle squeezed in next to Millie.

"No."

"Something went down." Annette pointed to yellow flags dotting the area.

"You're right." An oddly shaped chalk line was next to one of the flags.

"My first thought was that something had happened to Halbert. I'm glad to see he's all right." Cat glanced at her watch. "I need to head back to the ship to get ready for my day date with Andy."

"I'll go with you," Danielle said. "I need to catch up on some laundry."

"We'll let you know what we find out," Annette promised.

The crowd thinned, and Millie was finally able to catch Halbert's eye. He made his way over. "Hey, Millie."

"Hello, Halbert. What's going on?"

"The Southampton Strangler struck again." Halbert told Millie and Annette he could've sworn he saw the strangler the previous night. "I'm almost sure it was him. If only I had a way to call the police, this may have been prevented."

Millie and Annette exchanged a quick glance. One of Halbert's farewell gifts would take care of that problem.

"He murdered Clarissa Sinclair." Halbert eyed them expectantly.

Annette shaded her eyes, watching as Patterson stepped away from the others and began talking on his cell phone. "Who is Clarissa Sinclair?"

"A London socialite turned reporter."

"Interesting," Millie murmured. "So, perhaps she was investigating the strangler and ended up being his next victim."

"That's what I was thinking."

"I'm sorry to hear about such a sad ending to our time in Southampton," Millie said. "Now that we're here, are you ready to head over to the ship for our bon voyage party?"

A look of uncertainty clouded his face. "I-I was going to change my clothes."

Millie recognized the shirt and slacks he was wearing as ones she had given to him after cleaning out Nic's closet. "What you're wearing is just fine." She motioned toward the authorities, still gathered in a semi-circle. "Perhaps you should make sure the police don't need you any longer."

"Right." Halbert hurried toward them. After having a brief word, he returned. "They told me I could leave."

Millie guided Halbert out of the park, and Annette fell into step on the other side as they began making their way across the street to the security checkpoint.

She flashed her badge, briefly explaining she had obtained clearance from Donovan Sweeney to bring Halbert on board the ship.

"Ah." The guard grinned. "Halbert's getting the VIP treatment today."

"I am." The old man smiled back. "I'm gonna miss you, Kev."

The guard's smile vanished as he motioned toward the commotion across the street. "I heard the strangler struck again."

"It appears that way. I'm gonna miss you, my friend. Stay safe."

They passed through the gate and Halbert greeted several more members of the ship's security team, friends he had made and crewmembers who had made it a point to check on the homeless man during their months in port.

Suharto waved the trio through as they made their way up the ship's gangway. Once on board, Annette and Halbert stepped into the elevator while Millie darted up the stairs, reaching the elevator doors as they opened.

Halbert's jaw dropped, his eyes wide as he gazed around in wonderment. "This is the bee's knees. I always imagined what the inside of a fancy cruise ship might look like." He ran his fingertips along the polished handrail as his eyes traveled to one of the ship's twinkling chandeliers at the end of the corridor. "I cannot even imagine living on board this luxury liner. Thank you for inviting me."

"You've been like our guardian angel, watching over us this summer. Because of you, Sharky has Finn and we have a new friend." Millie eased the galley's swinging door open and led him inside while Annette brought up the rear.

Sharky, Finn and several of the security guards Halbert had befriended, along with Oscar, Patterson's right-hand man, were waiting inside.

Amit stood in front of the counter, which was filled with food. "Welcome to Annette's galley, Halbert."

Halbert hesitated, taking in the crisp, white linen tablecloths, the clusters of colorful balloons, the side table filled with drinks, surrounded by crewmembers who were there to say goodbye to their friend. "What..."

"The party is for you, our fond farewell to the British Isles and to our friend, Halbert." Millie patted his arm. "We will miss you."

"Yes," Oscar echoed. "You have become a friend, Halbert."

The old man's hand trembled as he rubbed the tip of his nose. "You've touched an old bloke's heart."

The guests feasted on hamburgers, hotdogs, and brats, crispy French fries, an array of creamy salads, chocolate chip cookies and parlies, a shortbread biscuit. There was tea, canned sodas, coffee and a Victoria sponge cake, a decadent dessert Annette had been perfecting during the season's teatime.

While they ate, Halbert's friends presented him with gifts, special mementos, each as individual and thoughtful as the giver.

Annette and Amit's gift was a portable cooler, something they knew he could use since several of the dock area employees often stopped by Halbert's place to drop off food and bottled water.

Sharky's gift was a handheld crank radio with a flashlight. "This is from Finn 'n me. If it wasn't for you, I wouldn't have my sidekick."

"Who also helped rescue my pup, Scout, from the dognappers," Millie reminded him. Her gifts were last, and she'd spent several days deciding what to give him, all items she was certain Halbert could use.

He teared up again when he unzipped the backpack and removed a package of socks, something Millie had purchased after discovering socks were one of the most requested items for the homeless.

There was also a new pair of tennis shoes, along with two fleece blankets, bottles of hand sanitizer, disposable wet wipes, a trio of toothbrushes, travel size tubes of toothpaste, boxes of Band-aids and rolls of toilet paper.

"This is so kind of everyone," Halbert's voice cracked. "I'm already blessed from having known all of you."

Millie swallowed hard. "I know this is a lot to carry, so I have a cart coming. We can load you up and then I'll walk you home. But first." Millie reached behind her for the small box, the final gift she had purchased for Halbert, something she hoped would not only make his life a little easier but also keep him safer. "This is for you."

The others grew quiet, already aware of what special gift Millie had picked out for her friend. Halbert slowly unwrapped the package. "What...what is this?"

"A phone. It's a cell phone—for you to keep in touch. I set up an account and will manage it for you. I already added my phone number."

"I don't know anyone, I mean, not anyone I could call to use the phone."

"You can call me." Millie paused, struggling to maintain her composure. "You can call and talk to any of us, and now you'll have a phone for emergencies, to keep you safe."

"Blimey. I don't know what to say." Halbert swiped at the tear that trickled down his cheek. "I've never had friends like this before."

Halbert proudly showed the cell phone off to his friends. Millie had written his number on a sticker and attached it to the back of the phone. He called her over. "Can you help me put in some phone numbers?"

"Of course." Millie stood next to him, entering the phone numbers of the crewmembers who promised to stay in touch.

Sharky and Finn were among the last to leave. "Halbert, my man, I don't know how I can ever thank you enough for giving Finn a place to stay until Millie brought him on board the ship. I'll never forget you."

"Finn is a good mouser. I would've kept him but Gus and him didn't hit it off."

Sharky gave Halbert his cell phone number and shook his hand before turning to Millie. "You gonna be around for a while?"

"I'm going to help Halbert take his gifts back to the warehouse, but it shouldn't take too long. Is your super-duper exciting surprise arriving soon?" she teased.

Sharky patted his radio. "It just arrived. I'm dropping Finn-meister off at home and then heading down to the dock so I can coordinate the unloading."

"I can't wait to see it."

Sharky sidled up to Annette, giving her googly eyes. "Would you like to check out my sweet surprise?"

"Check out your sweet surprise?" Annette snorted. "I'll pass."

"You could at least go down to see what it is," Millie chimed in. "Aren't you curious to find out what Sharky's surprise is?"

Annette pinched her index finger and thumb together. "My level of interest is about the size of a mustard seed."

"You can go, Miss Annette. I have the kitchen under control," Amit said.

"I suppose." Annette sucked in a breath. "Okay, I'll admit I'm more than a smidgen curious. Let me get the party stuff cleaned up. I'll meet you on the dock in fifteen."

Sharky helped Halbert and Millie load up the cart and then accompanied them as far as deck one, where he and Finn parted ways with them.

During the walk to Halbert's warehouse, he removed his cell phone from his pocket several times to admire it. "I've been thinking...I have a niece who used to live in nearby Midanbury. I might see if I can find someone to help me track down her telephone number."

"I can help you." They reached Halbert's warehouse and unloaded his gifts. Millie removed her cell phone from her pocket and began searching for Eloise, his niece's number. "I found an Eloise Kingswell in Midanbury."

"That's her." Halbert's eyes lit. "Can you write her number on a piece of paper?"

"I'll do one better. Give me your phone."

Halbert handed Millie his new phone, and she showed him how to add a contact.

"Look at all the people I can call." Halbert began counting as he scrolled through the list.

Millie spent the next several minutes showing him how to pull up the names and numbers, how to listen to his messages, and then delete them.

"I'll try not to spend too much time on the phone," Halbert promised.

"You can use it whenever you want." Millie explained she'd purchased an unlimited calling plan.

"That must cost a lot of money."

"The cost was reasonable. Besides, it will be worth the peace of mind knowing you're safe and able to reach someone if you need help." It was time for Millie to say goodbye to her friend, and she could feel her throat clog again at the thought. "We'll talk soon."

"Can I call you tomorrow?"

"Absolutely. If I don't answer leave a message, and I'll call you back."

"Thanks again, Millie."

"You're welcome." They reached the entrance, and she impulsively hugged him. "You take care of yourself, Halbert."

"I will, Millie. Me and Gus, we'll be just fine."

She gave him one final wave before making her way along the dock. When she turned back, he was still standing there, a sad smile on his face as he waved his new phone in the air.

The guard at the gate stopped her. "Gonna be sad to see the last of Halbert. Do you think we'll be back here again next summer, Millie?"

"I would like to think so, but from what I'm hearing, the answer is no."

"And you would know."

Millie reached the loading area. A wooden crate dangled from a yellow crane. A large white sticker with "this side up" in bold red letters caught her eye.

Sharky, sporting a hardhat and holding a megaphone, stood nearby, barking orders. "To the left. No. A little to the right. Watch it! You're letting it down too fast."

She spied Annette and Donovan Sweeney, the ship's purser, standing off to the side and wandered over. "Well?"

"I'm getting ready to take his megaphone away from him," Donovan said. "He's making the delivery guys nervous."

"Back this way. Easy...easy...and...we have it."

As soon as the crate was on the ground, Sharky snatched a crowbar from a maintenance worker's hand and wedged the flat end under the top.

"I'll be right back." Donovan eased past the women and approached Sharky.

The two appeared to have a heated exchange, and then Donovan rejoined them. "Sorry about that. Sharky needed a little reeling in."

"He's been talking about this for days now," Millie said.

"Days? More like weeks," Donovan said. "Honestly, I was surprised when corporate approved the expense. It cost Majestic Cruise Lines a pretty penny."

The sides of the crate were off now, and Millie glimpsed an oddly shaped object.

Sharky rubbed his hands together as he circled it several times. He plucked a box cutter from his pocket and began making a long slit in the cover. He walked to the other side and made another cut. With the help of one of the maintenance guys, he carefully removed what was left of the protective cover.

Annette's eyes narrowed. "What is it?"

"I still can't tell." Finally, Sharky and the worker stepped away, and Millie was able to get a clear and unobstructed view. "I'll be darned."

Chapter 3

Millie circled what was left of the crate. "What is this?"

"It's a Quadski, an amphibious vehicle. I call it the PRV—a personal rescue vehicle." Sharky ran a light hand along the shiny yellow hood. "This particular model is a high-tech, smaller version of a duck boat, part jet ski and part quad."

"It will be used for water rescues," Donovan elaborated, "and will replace Sharky's scooter."

"Nope." Sharky shook his head. "I gotta keep the scooter as a backup. Now that I've seen it in person, it's a little too wide for some of the ship's narrower corridors."

"We made a deal," Donovan said. "Reef and night maintenance use one MOT and you use the other."

"MOT?" Millie asked.

"Mode of transportation."

"Reef and I will hammer out the details." Sharky began directing the men standing nearby. They loaded the PRV onto a large cart and wheeled it toward the gangway.

Millie cringed, watching as the Quadski slowly made its way up the ramp. It squeezed through the opening with barely an inch of clearance on either side.

With the crewmember entrance now completely blocked, Suharto ran to the bottom of the gangway and began directing returning crewmembers to the passenger entrance at the other end.

"That's cool." Millie said. "I can't wait to see it in action."

Annette tilted her head. "I have a question. How are you gonna launch that thing in the water if we're in the middle of the ocean?"

"I'm glad you asked. Follow me." Donovan led the women along the dock to the bow of the ship. A large flat deck, supported by two thick black cables, jutted out of the side. "Check this out." He signaled to a crewmember standing on the deck.

The deck slowly lowered. It stopped, and then an inflatable ramp rolled out, flowing down into the water.

Annette let out a low whistle. "That's James Bond-ish slick."

Burum. Burum. The sound of an engine echoed from within the ship. Seconds later, Sharky and the PRV appeared.

"There he is. Are you going to let him take it out?"

"Not here," Donovan said. "There are too many ships and boats in the harbor. He'll have to wait until we're in open water."

"I think he has other plans," Annette said.

Sure enough, Sharky was easing the vehicle onto the deck.

"Hey!" Donovan made a timeout with his hands.

Sharky's face fell as he began backing the new rescue vehicle away from the inflatable ramp.

"I need to remind him of our agreement before he convinces the guys to let him take it out." Donovan sucked in a breath. "I hope I don't live to regret this decision."

Millie watched as the ship's purser hurried off. He ran into Dave Patterson near the gangway, and they had a brief word before both hustled back on board.

"That was interesting." Annette dusted her hands. "Hopefully, we'll never have to use it."

"I have to say, it's ingenious." Millie flung a light arm across Annette's shoulders as they trailed behind Donovan and boarded the ship. "Think of how much easier it will be to maneuver a smaller craft in the event of an emergency."

Back inside, Annette returned to the galley, while Millie made her way to Andy's office. She found her boss seated at his desk. "What are you still doing here? I thought you and Cat were heading out."

"In a few minutes." Andy tidied a stack of papers. "I was going over the passenger manifest. Siren of the Seas will be at capacity for the return voyage."

Millie had heard from several of the guests during their repositioning voyage that they would be returning to Miami at the end of the season.

"And some of them are passengers who made the trip over with us. It should be exciting." She changed the subject. "It appears the Southampton Strangler has struck again."

"I heard. What does this make now...three or four victims?" Andy asked.

"Three confirmed, at least according to what Halbert said."

"Speaking of Halbert, how was the party?"

"It was nice. It was also sad. I'm going to miss him. He loves the phone."

"You have a good heart."

Millie leaned her hip against the doorway. "What about you? Are you sad we're leaving?"

"I have mixed emotions. Although I'll miss my sister, Sarah, Siren of the Seas is my home."

Millie nodded, understanding exactly what Andy meant. Michigan would always be home-home. But the ship, the crew, not to mention Nic, had captured her heart, and it was where she was meant to be. "Where are you taking Cat?"

"Ah." Andy wagged his finger. "I can't divulge that information. Let's just say, it will be an adventure."

"I hope you have fun." Millie turned to go and then paused. "I'm happy for you, Andy. Happy for you and Cat."

"Me too, Millie. To think for years now, Cat has been right there, right under my nose, and I didn't even see her until I really looked."

"Love can be a fickle thing." Millie headed out to make her rounds. She swung by Sharky's office first and found him, along with several of his maintenance men, tinkering with the PRV. Reef, the night supervisor, was there too.

She caught Sharky's eye before making her way over.

"Well? What do you think?" he asked.

"It's very cool. I can't wait to see it in action. I mean, test mode. Not action, action."

Sharky licked his finger and swiped at a small smudge. "What do you think about me adding racing stripes, like the ones I have on my scooter?"

Millie wrinkled her nose. "Will Donovan let you alter the PRV?"

"I didn't plan on asking him. Why would he care about a few stickers?"

"The first thought that comes to mind is because this is a company asset and not personal property."

A flicker of hesitation crossed Sharky's face. "Yeah. Maybe you're right."

"So." Millie pointed to the scooter parked in the corner. "What happens to your scooter?"

"Sharky's giving it to me," Reef said.

"*Loaning* it to you," Sharky corrected. "It's a loaner. Besides, we're sharing it."

"Fine." Reef rolled his eyes. "You're sharing it."

"Donovan said you won't be testing it until we reach open water. I wouldn't mind seeing you and the PRV in action."

Sharky promised he would let her know when, and then Millie headed out. Her next stop was the apartment where Scout, her small Yorkie, stood waiting by the door.

Millie scooped him up and carried him onto the balcony. The port was bustling with stevedores, buzzing back and forth, loading boxes and bins.

Her eyes were drawn to Halbert's warehouse. From her vantage point, she could see the entrance to Queen's Park. The police cars were gone now, and she said a small prayer for the woman who had died.

Her concern for Halbert came flooding back, and she consoled herself with the fact he would now have a way to get help, if needed. "All right, Scout. It's time to get back to work. How would you like to tag along while I do a final check of the Welcome Aboard show I'm co-hosting?"

Ever since Scout's recent kidnapping, Millie had been careful to keep close tabs on the pup whenever they left the apartment. And because there weren't any passengers boarding yet, she figured it would be the perfect opportunity for him to get some fresh air.

Millie gave Nic, who was seated at the conference table, a quick wave as they crossed the bridge.

The Paradise Lounge was already buzzing with activity as crewmembers worked to set up tables for the Platinum Elite Diamond Welcome Aboard reception. Andy had gone all out by arranging for gourmet treats and premium beverages.

Millie looked forward to the VIP guest parties and, over the years, had gotten to know several Siren of the Seas' frequent cruisers.

After answering several questions, they headed upstairs to the lido deck to complete the sail away preparations. Everywhere they went, they were met with smiling faces. Like Millie, the crew had enjoyed their British Isles adventure, but they were ready to head home.

Kevin, one of the dancers, waved to Millie and then motioned for her to join him on the stage.

"Hello, Scout." Kevin patted the pup's head, and he rewarded him with a hand lick.

"How's it going?"

"We've had some minor technical difficulties with the sound equipment. Maintenance is working on it now." Kevin rubbed his hands together. "How does almost two weeks of nonstop entertainment sound?"

"Like a lot of fun and a lot of work." Millie chuckled. "At least this time I know what I'm getting myself into."

They chatted briefly, and then Millie kept moving. She went from top to bottom, stem to stern, ensuring the entertainment staff had everything they needed for the long-haul home.

She finished in time to drop Scout off at the apartment and then made her way down to the lobby to greet the arriving passengers. There was a buzz of anticipation in the air, from the staff at the guest services desk to the excursion desk crew to the cleaners, the bar staff, and everyone in between.

Andy was already waiting near the passenger entrance when Millie arrived. She eased in next to him. "How was your afternoon?"

"Fabulous." Andy tapped the tip of his nose. "I got a little too much sun."

"So...what did you do?"

"I chartered a sailboat."

Millie arched a brow. "You went sailing?"

"Sort of. I would call it more of a romantic escape for two, including a specially prepared lunch." Andy placed both hands behind his back and lifted his chin as he peered down at her. "It was quite lovely, if I do say so myself."

"I'm sure it was."

Their conversation ended when Suharto signaled the Platinum Elite Diamond passengers were making their way up the ramp.

Millie heard their excited chatter, and then the passengers began pouring into the atrium while a fleet of servers passed out flutes of champagne.

There were several familiar faces. Two of them were a couple Millie remembered meeting during their voyage to Southampton. Although their first names eluded her, she could remember the last.

"Mr. and Mrs. Ponsford." Millie smiled widely. "You're joining us for the return voyage?"

"Edward and Annabel," the woman corrected. "There's no need to be so formal, Millie. We've decided to spend a few months at our holiday home in Clermont. The grandchildren will be arriving via plane for a visit to Disney World during Christmas break." Several passengers gathered behind them, and Annabel introduced their friends, who were also traveling to their holiday homes.

After the introductions, the others began making their way to the servers.

"I'll be right there, Edward." Annabel lightly touched her necklace as she watched her husband trail behind their traveling companions. "We almost didn't board today after the tragic news of Clarissa Sinclair's death."

"The socialite who was also a news reporter?" Millie asked.

"Part-time news reporter," Annabel said. "Clarissa was to be on this cruise with us, to spend some time at her holiday home in the States, as well."

Chapter 4

Millie stared at Annabel. "The woman whose body was found in Queen's Park was booked on this voyage?"

"She was a friend of Edward's family." Annabel glanced over her shoulder and lowered her voice. "Not close to us, but she was traveling with us as a part of our group."

The woman's comment struck Millie as somewhat odd that a traveling companion was murdered, and the group decided to continue on with their plans.

As if reading Millie's mind, the woman continued. "I know it might come across as callous, but Ms. Sinclair was better acquainted with my sister-in-law. She and her husband are staying behind. In fact, Victoria, Edward's sister, is understandably distraught beyond measure."

Millie said the first thing that came to mind. "I'm sorry for your loss."

"Thank you." Annabel straightened her shoulders. "We'll get through it. It's good to see you again, Millie."

"Same here." Millie didn't have time to dwell on the discovery as more VIP passengers arrived. There was a brief break before the gold cardholders, followed by the silver and then blue, arrived. Last, but not least, were the first-time cruisers. Not surprisingly, there were only a handful.

Seasoned cruisers, those who were on board to enjoy the ship and its amenities and not as concerned about the itinerary and shore excursions, booked most of the repositioning / longer voyages.

The embarkation process flowed smoothly, and soon Suharto was signaling for the ship's crew to pull the gangway.

The door started to close. Millie's eyes were drawn to the dock and port that had become so familiar. It was a bittersweet moment, and she wondered if she would ever visit this special place again.

A signal sounded, followed by the announcement of the ship's muster drill.

Millie shifted into high gear as she made her way to her assigned muster station. The drill went off without a hitch, and they finished in what was close to record time.

The VIP party was next, and Millie headed home to freshen up.

She found Nic standing on the balcony. He was on his cell phone, and he held up a finger as she drew closer. "I see. I expect a full report will be sent to me, as well. We've already supplied the authorities with the names of the passengers who were linked to Ms. Sinclair's booking. Yes, I see. I look forward to an update soon."

Millie waited for Nic to end the call. "The woman they found in Queen's Park was booked on this voyage." She briefly filled him in on her conversation with Annabel Ponsford, how she and her husband, along with some others, were traveling with the woman.

"The authorities have interviewed each person in the group. They requested a copy of the ship's manifest, to cross-reference persons of interest." Nic explained there had been several possible strangler sightings in the Southampton area during the past couple of days. "They believe he was hanging around the port for a reason."

Millie thought about what Halbert had said. "It makes me wonder if Sinclair knew the strangler or if it was a case of being in the wrong place at the wrong time."

"Again, there are a lot of unanswered questions." Nic's jaw tightened. "Unfortunately, the timing of her death is a concern. The authorities had no grounds to detain Sinclair's traveling companions. We were unable to delay departure. We have a sold-out cruise booked out of Miami as soon as we return." He started to say something and abruptly stopped.

"What is it?"

"They are leaning toward thinking there's a solid chance the serial killer boarded the ship."

"Because the strangler was silent for years until right after Siren of the Seas docked here for the season."

"They believe there may be some correlation." Nic glanced at his watch. "I'm meeting with Patterson and the security team, to fill them in on what we know as well as review our current security measures."

Millie's scheduler app chimed. "I need to get ready for the VIP shindig." She dashed up the stairs to their bedroom. When she emerged, Nic had already left. She passed through the bridge and discovered that the security meeting was already in progress.

With a few minutes to spare, Millie did a final quick check of the party's food and beverages. She caught up with Andy, who was in the back chatting with the members of the orchestra. "You did a jolly good job of organizing our VIP Welcome Aboard party, Millie."

"Thanks. The passengers are looking forward to this voyage. I wanted it to start off with a bang." Millie eyed a large purple bruise that was forming on the side of her boss's forehead. "What happened to your forehead?"

"I had a run in with the sailboat's boom while I was touring it. It was still dark when I met with the captain early this morning. I wasn't watching where I was going, and *boom*. I ran right into it."

"It looks like it's going to be a humdinger."

"I'll survive." Andy changed the subject. "I'm running late for an emergency meeting with the captain and ship's security team."

"It's already started. You had better get going." Millie followed Andy to the door, where she began collecting the VIP invitations.

Danielle passed her boss on his way out and hurried to the other side to help greet the guests and collect the invitations.

Millie worked quickly, welcoming each of them and thanking them for joining the staff and crew for the long voyage before directing them to the servers who were passing out cocktails along with small plates of savory treats.

The crowd cleared, and she cued Danielle to close the other entrance door. The orchestra warmed up, and Millie watched as the guests filled the dance floor.

"It looks inviting."

Millie turned to find her husband standing next to her. "Yes, it does. How did your meeting go?"

"Patterson is keeping in touch with the authorities in Southampton. We'll be among the first to hear if there are any updates."

"Good evening, Captain Armati, Mrs. Armati." A server stood directly behind Nic. "Can I entice you to try one of our savory dishes?"

Millie perused the offerings. "I haven't eaten since Halbert's luncheon. I went over the food and beverage list earlier, but why don't you tell the captain what you have."

"Of course." The tall blonde used her tongs to point out the various appetizers. "These are avocado-pesto BLT crackers. We also have artichoke wonton wrappers. If you like a little bite, there are bacon-wrapped jalapeño peppers. My favorite are the sun-dried tomato basil tortilla wraps."

"I'll try your favorite," Millie said.

"Make it two."

"Excellent choice." The server plucked napkins from the tray and placed two of the wraps on a plate. "It's a blend of cream cheese and Parmesan cheese, sun-dried tomatoes, chopped spinach, and minced garlic spread on a flour tortilla. The fresh basil gives it a unique taste."

Nic took a bite. "It's delicious. Thank you for the recommendation..."

"Joy. You're welcome. I love experimenting with different dishes." She leaned in and whispered conspiratorially. "The wraps were my idea."

"And spot on." Millie nibbled the end. "You must be new."

"Brand-spanking." Joy shifted the tray to her other hand. "I've been living abroad for several years, most recently in the UK and decided it was time to find a job closer to home."

"Where is home?"

"Divine, Kansas. Most people have never heard of it, although it's a national landmark. In fact, that's how I got my name. My parents thought it would be clever to tie my name into our little claim to fame. Joy from Divine." Joy explained it was smack dab in the middle of the contiguous United States. "A lot of tourists visit in the summer, which is how I got the travel bug. I worked as a summer tour guide and met all kinds of people from other parts of the country and world."

"Welcome to Siren of the Seas," Nic politely replied. "You'll meet some fascinating crew and passengers here, as well."

"Thank you, captain." Joy snapped to attention and saluted him. "I had better get back to work."

Millie watched as Joy approached a group of guests nearby. "I like her. She has spunk. It's also unusual to have an American server on board the ship."

The wait staff continued circling the room while Millie made her way to the stage to introduce the ship's officers. Her last introduction was Nic, who started off by making a small speech, welcoming the passengers and thanking them for their continued loyalty to Majestic Cruise Lines.

He presented several awards and gifts to the passengers celebrating milestone cruises before ending his part of the presentation. Patterson was waiting for him near the back, and Millie watched as he whispered something in her husband's ear before they slipped out of the room.

The orchestra started playing again, and the champagne flowed. Millie mixed and mingled, and then she spotted a familiar face.

She slipped past a large group near the center of the room and tapped Thomas Windsor on the shoulder. He spun around, his eyes lighting when he found her standing behind him. "Millie Armati."

"The Silver Fox is back on board," Millie quipped. "I didn't know you were traveling back to the States with us."

"No? I thought I mentioned it when we arrived in Southampton."

"If you did, it went right on by." Millie waved a hand over her head. "Did you enjoy your time in the UK?"

"I did. I took care of some loose ends regarding some family issues, tidying things up, if you will. At my age, who knows if I'll make it back again."

Millie touched his arm. "We're thrilled to have you back on board."

"Oh, we are too," the woman standing next to him gushed.

"Where are my manners?" Thomas turned to the others. "This is Bruce and Hilda Ellis, Harry and Kate Moxey, and Edward and Annabel Ponsford."

Millie's heart skipped a beat. This was the group who was traveling with Clarissa Sinclair, the part-time reporter whose body was found in the park.

Remembering Annabel's words, Millie was careful to avoid mentioning the woman's name. "We met earlier, during boarding," she explained. "Are you all traveling to your holiday homes?"

"We are," Kate said. "Bruce and Hilda recently retired and purchased a home in Florida."

"Sight unseen," Bruce Ellis added. "Leave it to my wife to get her hands on some money and it starts burning a hole in her pocket."

Hilda playfully punched him. "I haven't spent it all."

"Not yet."

"I'm the odd man out," Thomas said. "The only one without a vacation home."

"We're trying to convince Thomas to purchase a small holiday condo near us," Annabel said. "The ladies in our community would love to have him around in season."

"I'm sure the single ladies on board the ship will be thrilled, as well." Millie thanked them for cruising with them. She stepped away, her mind whirling.

Thomas had arrived in Southampton on board Siren of the Seas. Not long after, the strangler picked up where he left off, after lying low for almost five years. He was also acquainted with Clarissa Sinclair, or at least he knew *of* her.

The strangler had stayed close to the Southampton area. She remembered Thomas' comment, how he was taking care of some "loose ends." Was returning to Southampton to kill off several more women the reason for his return trip? Or the loose end?

"It can't be Thomas," Millie whispered under her breath. She pushed the disturbing thought from her mind as she continued making her rounds.

The party ended, and it was time for her to host karaoke, followed by a round of trivia. Up next was the Welcome Aboard show, and she had to hustle to make it to the theater on time.

She stood in the wings, watching as Andy started his spiel, giving them a brief rundown of the itinerary. Ten days in, they would spend the night in Bermuda and then finish the last leg of their trip, arriving at the Port of Miami in the early morning hours of day thirteen.

Each of the headliner entertainers gave the crowd a small sampling of what was to come. Siren of the Seas' singers and dancers took over, and the Welcome Aboard show ended in a rousing medley of rock and jazz with a touch of country mixed in.

Millie's scheduled break was sandwiched in between the dining room's second seating and the evening's late-night activities. She headed upstairs to the Waves Buffet to grab a bite to eat and found a quiet spot, which wasn't hard. The dining room was nearly empty.

"Hey." Millie looked up to find Danielle hurrying toward her. "Is it your dinner break too?"

"Yep. I love the excitement of embarkation day, but I have to say this one has been crazy."

"Mind if I join you?" Danielle placed her plate of food on the table. "I ran into Annette. She's over by the carving station and is going to join us."

"The more, the merrier."

Annette arrived a short time later. "Finally, a chance to sit down." She groaned loudly as she slid into an empty chair. "I knew I would pay for that long walk around Stonehenge."

"But it was worth it," Millie insisted.

"Every second." Annette unwrapped her silverware. "How's it going in your world?"

"Great. It's like meeting up with old friends. There are a lot of VIPs on board, not to mention a few passengers who were with us at the beginning of the season for the voyage over." Millie thought about Thomas Windsor. "Thomas Windsor is one of them."

"He is?" Danielle lifted a brow. "Thanks for the warning. The senior singles' parties should reach a whole new level of excitement with Thomas around."

"He's traveling with the crowd who was with Clarissa Sinclair."

"Why does that name sound familiar?" Annette asked.

"She's the woman, the part-time reporter, they found in Queen's Park this morning."

Annette made a choking sound. "The one they think was taken out by the strangler?"

"Yep." Millie shared what Nic had told her, that the authorities suspected the strangler might be on board the ship.

"Do you think there's a chance Thomas is the strangler?" Danielle asked in a low voice.

"I haven't had time to process it yet." Millie grabbed her fork and stabbed a piece of broccoli.

"The strangler was quiet for several years. The Siren of the Seas shows up—the strangler strikes again. Most of his victims were found near the port, including Clarissa, *and* Thomas is traveling with Clarissa's group." She remembered Thomas's odd comment about taking care of loose ends. "He told me he was in the UK to take care of some loose ends."

Annette rubbed the sides of her arms. "Wouldn't that be something?"

"I was thinking maybe I should swing by Patterson's office and at least mention what I've heard." A tinge of guilt filled Millie for suspecting Thomas of being the strangler. He was such a nice man and so thoughtful. "He's a great guy."

"Always suspect the least suspect," Danielle said. "He is popular with the women. Perhaps there was some trigger in his life that turned him into a psycho, and he kills women for kicks."

"And collects souvenirs," Millie reminded them. "The strangler has taken something from each of his victims. Regardless, I think it would be wise to be on guard."

The trio finished eating and parted ways, with Millie making a beeline for Patterson's office. His office door was locked, and the lights were off. The chat would have to wait.

Her long day finally ended with a quick check of the nightclub, and then she headed home. Nic was already there when she arrived. He was on the balcony with Scout napping in his lap.

"Hey," Millie whispered.

Scout woke at the sound of her voice, and she patted his head. "Even poor Scout is tuckered out."

"It was a long day." Nic waited for Millie to have a seat. "I heard from the investigator in charge of Clarissa Sinclair's case earlier this evening and discovered something interesting."

Chapter 5

"Clarissa Sinclair injured the strangler during her struggle to survive," Nic said.

Millie grew quiet as she processed the information. "How? Did they tell you what sort of injury?"

"No, and this is to be kept strictly confidential. I probably shouldn't have even mentioned it. The authorities don't want this information getting out."

"I have what I believe may be a person of interest." Millie briefly told Nic her suspicions, how Thomas Windsor had journeyed to Southampton on board Siren of the Seas. "I don't know what to make of it. The killer surfaced again after falling off the face of the earth. Factor in the fact most of the killings took place near the port *and* Thomas is traveling with Clarissa's group."

"It does seem to be an uncanny coincidence," Nic admitted. "I'm sure the authorities are looking into it."

While her husband got ready for bed, Millie thought about Thomas, about the strangler's victims, and the authorities' suspicions that the serial killer could be on board the ship.

She spent the night tossing and turning and woke early the next morning, her mind still on the strangler.

The longer voyages had a different feel than the other cruises, and repositioning cruises added an extra dimension to the passenger mindset. It was all about relaxing and being entertained.

Millie wasted no time showering and dressing. Her first stop was the early morning meeting with Andy and the entertainment staff. He addressed a handful of passenger issues and then reminded them it would be all hands on deck for the duration of the trip. "Our only break will be near the end when we stop in Bermuda overnight. I'll warn you right now the ship is at capacity, so I'm not approving time off."

There was an inaudible murmur among the staff, and Andy's eyes traveled around the room. "Dare I hear any complaints?"

"Complaints? No. Disappointment? A little," Felix said. "Bermuda isn't part of our normal itinerary."

"Bermuda is like any other island. It's tropical. There are palm trees and beaches."

"Party pooper," Felix mumbled under his breath.

"What did you say?" Andy's eyes narrowed.

"I said you're a good party planner."

"That's what I thought you said. You're dismissed. Now, get out there and make some fun."

Millie swung by the buffet to grab a container of yogurt and then ate it on her way to Sunrise Stride, the early risers trek around the jogging track. She ran into Annette, who was already on her second lap.

"I'm glad to see you're taking this getting-healthy-to-control-your-angina exercise routine seriously." Millie fell into step and picked up the pace.

"Me too," Annette said. "I'm no longer huffing and puffing, which is probably another reason I enjoyed yesterday's outing."

Millie changed the subject. "Nic heard back from the Southampton authorities. Clarissa, the strangler's most recent victim, injured him, or her, during her attack."

"No kidding. How do they know that?"

"The authorities aren't saying, at least not yet. Please don't mention this to anyone. They don't want this getting out to the public."

Annette made a zipping motion across her lips. "My lips are sealed. What does Patterson think?"

"He wasn't around last night, which reminds me I need to stop by his office this morning."

Several passengers joined them, and by their third lap around the track it was packed. She and Annette passed a few and were passed by others.

The sun was rising, and Millie could tell it was going to be a beautiful day—warm and sunny. It reminded her of the balmy Caribbean temperatures minus the humidity.

They finished their walk, and Annette and Millie stepped off to the side. "If you're interested, I'm tinkering with a new breakfast recipe and need some feedback."

Millie patted her stomach. "I had a container of yogurt earlier. What time?"

"Ten-thirty-ish," Annette said. "Midway between the breakfast and lunch crowd."

"I'll be there." Millie gave her a thumbs up before heading downstairs. Once again, Dave Patterson wasn't around, but Oscar was there. "Where's Patterson?"

"Making his rounds. He is very much..." Oscar paused as he struggled to find the right words. "Hands on for this voyage."

"Because of the strangler, not to mention the number of sea days," Millie guessed, and Oscar nodded. "We are a long way away from help if something happens."

"And there are only so many jail cells on board the ship."

"Yes. We always have one or two troublemakers."

Millie thanked him and then made her way to the lounge for morning trivia. Deciding to do something special, she ordered coffee and donuts, which were promptly delivered by one of Annette's galley crewmembers.

The server unloaded the tray on a nearby table, passing by the Ellises, a couple who were part of Clarissa's group. They found a table for two in a dark corner, and Mr. Ellis promptly pulled out his cell phone.

His wife began chatting with the couple next to them. Since the ship was spending most of the time at sea, Millie decided a trivia game about the ocean was a perfect fit and had even learned a thing or two while doing some online research.

The first was that the Atlantic Ocean was the second largest body of water, with the Pacific Ocean being the largest.

The final question was a fun fact, and Millie's favorite. "Here's my final and favorite question. Where can you find a peacock mantis shrimp?"

She finished timing the question and then stood. "Time's up. Swap answers with the group to your right."

When they finished, she made her way down the list. "Did anyone get the peacock mantis question—about where you can find them—correct?"

A few raised their hands. "The answer is the Indian and Pacific Oceans. It's a fascinating and colorful creature, able to punch hard enough to break glass in the blink of an eye."

She announced the winners and handed out Siren of the Seas' pens and discount coupons to the winners. Millie thanked them and began making her rounds, clearing the tables.

Hilda Ellis hurried toward her. "Hello, Millie."

"Hello, Mrs. Ellis." Millie offered the woman a smile. "Thank you for joining me."

"It was fun, but I was a little disappointed."

"Disappointed?"

"In your explanation of the peacock mantis shrimp. You could've taught the group a thing or two."

Hilda's husband wandered over, sporting the same sullen expression he was wearing when he arrived. "Let's go, Hilda. I'm hungry."

Hilda cast him an annoyed look. "Hang on a minute. As I was telling Millie, the mantis shrimp is fascinating. You should do a better job of researching your trivia."

"I did my research. I learned the shrimp is not only amazingly colorful and quick, punching fifty times faster than the blink of an eye, it's tiny, only a few inches in length."

"I also took issue with you not giving us a little more in-depth information about the Atlantic Ocean."

"I'm sorry you didn't enjoy the trivia," Millie apologized.

"Oh, I enjoyed it but thought it was a bit...lacking. I attended your trivia yesterday, and it seems to me you were a little more...shall we say, on your game?"

"On my game?" Millie sucked in a breath.

"You know." Hilda snapped her fingers. "Sharp."

"I see. Well, I shall try to up my game."

"When is the next round?"

"I don't know. I'm not hosting it."

"Let's go, Mrs. know-it-all." Bruce rolled his eyes as he placed a hand on his wife's back and propelled her out of the lounge.

Millie's stomach started to rumble, reminding her it was almost time to sample Annette's breakfast goodies. She finished putting the supplies in the closet and locked the door when her cell phone rang.

It was Halbert. She made her way to the window for clearer reception. "Hello, Halbert."

"Millie? Can you hear me?" Halbert's voice was faint, and she had to strain to hear him.

"I can hear you. You sound as if you're in a tunnel. How do you like your new phone?"

"It's great. I didn't mean to bother you but wanted to tell you I called my niece. She's picking me up and taking me to her house for dinner this evening."

"That's wonderful. I'm so happy for you."

"Thanks to you, Millie." There was a moment of silence. "I watched the ship leave port but couldn't bring myself to come out to wave goodbye. I figured maybe if I didn't wave goodbye, it would somehow mean one day you'll be back."

A lump lodged in her throat. "Look on the bright side, when I see you again, we'll have so much to catch up on." *If I see you again,* Millie silently added.

"Yes. I'll let you go. I just wanted to give you the exciting news."

"Thank you. We'll talk soon."

"Wait. I had something else to tell you. It's about the strangler."

Millie perked up. "What is it?"

"A dockhand was there right after the authorities showed up. He told me he overheard one of them say Clarissa fought the strangler and injured him during her attack."

"Do you know how she injured him?"

"Scratched 'em with her fingernails. He also said her glasses were missing. She wore prescription glasses. There's one other thing," Halbert said. "They think the strangler may have boarded your ship."

"I heard the same."

"Be careful, Millie."

"I will. Thank you, Halbert. We'll all be careful."

After ending the call, Millie stared at the phone. There had to be a reason the authorities believed the strangler was on board the ship, which meant they knew more than Nic or the ship's security team, but were withholding their findings.

Disturbed by Halbert's call and the increasing number of reports the killer was on board, Millie stopped by the apartment to grab her stun gun, something she hadn't kept on her for a long time. She checked the device to make sure it was operating properly and then headed to the galley for breakfast.

Cat was there, along with Danielle and Amit. Millie stepped inside, sniffing appreciatively. "Something smells delish."

"Bacon. I'm tweaking a bacon breakfast pizza."

"You had me at bacon." Millie hopped onto the barstool, hungrily eyeing the dishes on the counter. "What's in it besides bacon?"

Annette finished slicing the pieces and grabbed a spatula. "Sautéed onions, red bell pepper, cheese and pizza crust." She placed a wedge on Millie's plate while Amit went along behind her and added a scoop of fresh fruit on the side.

After portioning out the samples, Annette fixed a plate for her and Amit. She sawed off the tip. "Bon appétit."

Millie studied her wedge before taking a big bite. She let out a moan of pure delight. "This tastes as good as it smells."

"Here, here." Danielle picked up her piece and bit the end. "I love pizza. I love bacon and combining the two for breakfast is sheer bliss."

"It is," Cat agreed. "Are you thinking about adding it to the breakfast menu?"

"No. I'm adding it to the brunch menu."

"It's a winner." Millie gave a thumbs up before nudging Cat. "So, how did the date day go?"

"It was wonderful." Cat's faced turned a tinge of pink. "It would have been even better if the cops hadn't stopped me and Andy on our way back to the ship."

"The police detained you?" Annette asked.

"Andy." Cat explained Andy had gotten off the ship early the previous morning to meet with the sailboat's captain to pay for and arrange the final details. "He passed by the park before the authorities found Clarissa's body, and they wanted to know if he'd seen or heard anything."

"Obviously, he hadn't," Danielle said. "Otherwise, I'm sure he would've reported it."

"Yeah. It was kinda crazy. Once they found out he was British, they really started grilling him."

Millie grew quiet. Andy hadn't mentioned being detained by the police. He was British. He was familiar with the UK. *No, Millie,* she silently chided herself. *There's no way Andy is the Southampton Strangler.* "It can't be Andy. He's been out of the country."

Annette leaned an elbow on the counter. "I'm not saying Andy is the strangler, not by a longshot, but I get where the authorities might want to take a closer look at him. Think about it. He's British. He returned to the UK around the time the strangler started striking again. He was in the area of where the last woman's body was found."

"What about the other incidents?" Millie was certain the ship was somewhere else when Edith Branson, the first victim, not to mention the young woman from "uni" was murdered...or was it? "I'm sure the authorities cleared Andy from suspicion."

Cat wrinkled her nose.

"You think they seriously suspect him?" Danielle asked.

"I think he's a person of interest, and so does he."

"He got a clunk on the head. He has a real shiner from being hit by the sailboat's boom," Cat said.

Millie remembered what Nic had told her, how the authorities believed the latest victim had fought back and the strangler had been injured. Halbert mentioned Clarissa scratching her killer. What if she had not only scratched her killer but also conked him in the head?

If Millie were in a life and death battle, she would fight with everything she had, which is what Clarissa had done. And left her mark.

"I have some pictures of our sailing adventure."

The others gathered around Cat as she turned her cell phone on and began scrolling through the pictures. The first was of them boarding the sailboat.

Cat had taken a picture of the tantalizing tray of goodies. It warmed Millie's heart when she saw the picture of them cuddled up together.

There was one more of them lounging in the sun, a silly grin on Andy's face as Cat leaned in to whisper in his ear.

There was something else in the picture Millie noticed...bright, red scratches on his arm.

Chapter 6

Millie's heart skipped a beat. "Poor Andy. First, he clunks his head and then he ends up with nasty scratches on his arm."

"Scratches?" Cat reached for her phone. "I never noticed them yesterday."

"I gotta get going." Danielle hopped off her stool. "Thanks for the delicious breakfast, Annette."

"I need to head out, too. I'm hosting a ship tour, and it includes a stop by the captain's apartment, so I want to make sure it's tidy."

Annette began stacking the dirty dishes. "I wouldn't like that, not one bit. I wouldn't put it past some of the female passengers who become enamored by the thought of a romantic fling with the ship's captain to try something sneaky."

"Like hide in our coat closet and pounce on Nic when he comes home?" Millie joked.

"I'm serious. They see a handsome man in uniform and go nuts."

"Some of them do get a little...shall we say, enthusiastic about Nic."

Annette batted her eyes and patted her chest. "A man in uniform. Maybe I should hide in the captain's closet and surprise him when he comes home."

"You're hilarious." Millie chuckled. "I already have them leaving him notes, inviting him back to their cabin. You're going to have me checking the bedroom closets at night."

"Better safe than sorry."

"True. I'll see you in a few. I would like to start the tour here if you don't mind."

"Not at all."

Millie hustled home for a quick inspection, making sure their private quarters were shipshape. On her way back out, she gave Nic a heads up she was bringing the tour group through.

Several passengers were already waiting at the designated spot near guest services when she arrived. Millie's heart sank when she discovered Hilda and Bruce Ellis were a part of the group.

She waited until the last person on her list arrived and then gave them an overview of the areas they would be visiting. As promised, she started the tour in the galley by introducing them to Annette.

She stood near the back, listening while Annette spouted off some interesting facts about the amount of food consumed on board the ship during a typical seven-day cruise before showing them the freezers, the refrigerators, and the prep area. She finished by giving them a tour of each of the stations.

Millie knew trouble was brewing when Hilda pulled a notepad from her pocket and flipped it open. "I read on your website there are eighteen kitchens on board this ship."

"There are eighteen galleys on board Siren of the Seas. This is the largest galley, serving all the main dining rooms," Annette explained.

"Will we be touring the others?" Hilda asked.

"No," Millie answered.

"Why not?"

"Because it would take all day to visit all the galleys." Millie forced a smile. "Shall we move on?" She thanked Annette for the tour and then led the group out into the corridor.

Their second stop was the theater's backstage where Andy was waiting. He led them to the dressing rooms, the costume closets, and the costume repair area, all the while spouting off tidbits and fun facts about not only the productions and performers but also the cost of the costumes.

Up next was the engine room, which wasn't far from the laundry center, another part of the tour, before they made the trek up the steps to the bridge.

Both Nic and Captain Vitale were on hand. Millie introduced them before stepping off to the side.

Nic caught his wife's eye and winked before addressing the group.

"Welcome to Siren of the Seas' bridge." He gave them the ship's position, their current speed, and the number of nautical miles traveled since leaving Southampton. He answered several questions before Millie continued their tour by leading them down the hall to their private quarters.

Scout was waiting inside. She scooped him up and then held the door for the others. "For security and privacy, I'll only be showing you the kitchen, the dining room, living room and the apartment's balcony."

Hilda and her husband, Bruce, brought up the rear.

"What a cute little pup." Hilda patted his head. "I didn't know dogs were allowed on board the ship."

"They're not. Scout is an exception. He's Captain Armati's dog."

"Bending the rules for the captain?" Hilda curled her lip.

"Hilda," her husband scolded. "It's none of your business."

"Just making a comment," she airily replied as she strolled into the living room. "This is larger than I thought it would be."

"The apartment is approximately eleven hundred square feet. There is one bedroom and two bathrooms. As I mentioned, we'll only be touring the kitchen, along with the dining and living room areas."

"This isn't really a behind-the-scenes tour if we can't see it all," Hilda sniffed.

"The captain's bedroom suite is off limits," Millie bluntly replied.

Hilda's sharp eye took it all in. "I thought it would be more masculine. I see a woman's touch." She pivoted, eyeing Millie. "Is the captain married?"

"He is."

"Does his wife live on board the ship?"

"She does. She works for Siren of the Seas, as well."

"What does she do?" Hilda asked.

"She's the assistant cruise director."

A man in the group chuckled. "You're the assistant cruise director, Millie."

"I'm also Captain Armati's wife."

Hilda eyed Millie with renewed interest. "You don't seem the captain's wife type."

"I think you're an adorable couple," a woman gushed. "He's so tall and handsome. I must say that you have the dream life, the dream job, the dream husband."

"I am a very blessed woman," Millie said. "As far as the living arrangements, as you can well imagine, we spend little time here. Most of our meals are squeezed in between our busy schedules. Nic spends most of his time on the bridge. The proximity of our home to the bridge is a necessity."

"The poor little pup." Hilda tsk-tsked. "He's stuck inside the apartment."

"Scout accompanies me to a number of events and when I make my rounds around the ship."

"He's so tiny. Aren't you afraid he'll get lost?"

No matter what she said, she couldn't win. Millie resisted the urge to roll her eyes. "Let's keep moving."

She led the group out of the apartment, across the bridge and to the guest services desk, where they started their tour. Millie had radioed ahead, and Donovan was there to meet them and wrap up the tour.

The group began drifting away until only Hilda and her husband remained.

"Did you enjoy the tour?"

Hilda opened her mouth to speak. Bruce was quick to cut her off. "Very much so, Millie. We had no idea you were the captain's wife. The behind-the-scenes tour was fantastic, and you showed us many areas we never would've seen."

"What was your favorite?"

"The engine room."

"Mine was the tour of the bridge and a glimpse of your apartment," Hilda said. "Although I think you should've told us up front, you were the captain's wife."

Millie lifted a brow. "Would it have made a difference?"

"Not at all." Bruce grasped his wife's arm. "I'm sure Millie has other events to attend to. Thanks again."

"You're welcome." As they walked off, Millie couldn't help but feel a smidgen sorry for Hilda's husband.

With the tour out of the way, Millie headed to the pool bar to meet with the Cruise Clue participants, the ship's adult scavenger hunt. Cruise Clue was one of Millie's favorites, and even more so since Andy had given her free rein to pick the clues.

She'd added several new—and trickier—ones. While the group dashed out to begin their hunt, Millie sipped an iced tea and chatted with the bar staff.

The timed event flew by and when all groups were accounted for, she tallied the total, tickled to discover none of the groups had found all the items.

She finished awarding the prizes when her radio went off. "Millie, do you copy?"

"Go ahead, Sharky."

"Where are you?"

"Near the pool deck bar. I just finished my scavenger hunt. Why? What's up?"

"I'm taking the PRV out for a test run."

"With Donovan's permission?" Millie asked.

"Of course. Your hubby, the captain, even slowed the ship for us."

Millie had noticed the ship was barely moving, and briefly wondered if something had happened. "I'm up for a break."

"Cool. Meet me on crew deck zero."

"Aye. Aye. I'm on my way." Millie scrambled down the stairs, stopping when she reached the galley.

Annette was inside and standing near the counter. "Hey, Millie. Don't tell me you have another VIP tour."

"Nope. Sharky's getting ready to launch his PRV and invited me to check it out."

"This oughta be good." Annette wiped her hands. "Hey, Amit."

Amit, who was near the dessert prep area, hustled across the galley. "Yes?"

"You wanna take a quick break with Millie and me and check out Sharky's new toy?"

"His PRV?"

"Yep. He's getting ready to launch it."

"It sounds very exciting. I am ready."

On the way down, Millie radioed Danielle and invited her to join them.

When they arrived, they found a large crowd of the ship's crewmembers had already gathered. Not only was the maintenance staff on hand, Donovan,

Dave Patterson and Doctor Gundervan were also there.

Millie bounced on the tips of her toes, watching as the crewmember on the right pressed a round, red button. The inflatable ramp she'd seen the previous day began filling with air. As it filled, it unfolded and slowly lowered into the water.

A horn honked, and the crowd parted, making way for Sharky and his Quadski. He was grinning from ear to ear as he sat atop the PRV. He revved the engine as he drew closer, forcing Donovan to give him a warning shake of the head.

Millie was too far away to hear what he said, but Sharky cooled his jets and the vehicle slowed. He stopped near the top of the ramp and then hopped off.

The vehicle reminded Millie of a smaller version of an ATV four-wheeler. The fiberglass frame was bright yellow. A black box was attached to the back.

Donovan cleared his throat. "I know you're all curious about this new rescue vehicle. It's a Quadski or, as Sharky likes to call it, a PRV, personal rescue vehicle." He explained to the group they would use it for not only water rescues, but to reach shore in tendering ports in the event of an emergency. "This is a first for Majestic Cruise Lines and something which will be rolled out to the rest of the fleet if it works well for Siren of the Seas."

"It's history in the making." Sharky finished his inspection and climbed back on. He pulled on a pair of goggles before giving everyone a thumbs up.

Wah. Wah. Millie covered her ears as Sharky revved up the motor. The PRV crept forward. It jostled back and forth as it made its way down the inflatable ramp.

"I wonder how they'll handle a night rescue," Millie said aloud.

Reef, who was standing nearby, pointed to a set of double floodlights hanging near the hatch. "We installed a set on each side. One light is pointed down at the ramp and another out into the water."

"You guys thought of everything," Annette said.

"Sharky. He's gonna do a little more tweaking with Donovan's permission, of course." Reef tapped the side of his forehead. "As soon as Sharky found out the PRV was on order, he started researching it. I don't think he even slept last night."

"Where's Finn?" Millie glanced around, looking for Sharky's sidekick, the stray cat she had rescued from Halbert's warehouse.

"He's in the office," Reef said. "He's kinda skittish around the PRV. Besides, Sharky has to add Finn's basket and Donovan hasn't given him the approval yet."

Reef nodded toward the hatch door. "There he goes."

Millie craned her neck, watching as Sharky gunned the PRV and shot off the end of the ramp. A tail of water flew behind him as he leaned in and spun in a wide circle. He jumped his wake, gunning the engine and spraying the men who were standing in the doorway.

"Jerk!" one of them yelled as he swiped at his face.

Sharky did another pass by and Millie noticed the PRV's tires were turned on their side. She nudged Annette. "Check out the tires."

"I've never seen anything like it before in my life."

Donovan whistled and motioned to Sharky, waving him back to the ship.

"Yes, sir."

"It's time for you to stage a rescue," Donovan said.

"I need a volunteer." Sharky shoved his goggles up.

Half a dozen of the crewmembers raised their hands.

Millie shrank back.

But it was too late. "I pick Millie."

"No." She shook her head. "I'm not dressed for the water."

Donovan chuckled. "I think you should try it, Millie."

"My uniform will get ruined."

Sharky snapped his fingers. "Reef, go grab the new waterproof suit."

Reef ran down the hall and returned holding a rubber yellow suit. "This came with the Quadski. It's waterproof and even has a hood to keep your hair dry."

"No." Millie began backing away as she shook her head.

"C'mon Millie," Sharky said. "It'll be fun."

"Yeah," Danielle laughed. "Go for it, Millie."

"I'm with Danielle," Annette said. "It'll be a blast."

"Millie. Millie," Sharky chanted, and soon the others joined in until it was a loud chorus of "Millie."

"All right, but I'm holding you personally responsible if this test run goes south." Millie reluctantly took the wetsuit from Reef and began pulling it on. A plastic zipper ran up the center and elastic cuffs circled both wrists and ankles.

She slid the hoodie on and tucked her hair inside before securing it with the Velcro chin strap. Millie slipped on the lifejacket Reef handed her, adding a puffy layer of bright orange that contrasted the yellow. "I'm a yellow duck in a lifejacket."

"I gotta get a picture of this." Annette snatched her cell phone from her pocket, aiming it at Millie. "Smile."

"No."

"Okay, then look cranky," Annette joked.

"You look cute." Danielle tugged on the safety strap. "Yellow is your color. I think we should post a picture of you and Sharky on the employee bulletin board."

Millie stuck her tongue out. "Very funny."

"Daylight is burning." Donovan propelled Millie toward the inflatable ramp.

She hovered near the edge, waiting for Sharky to coast to the side of the ship.

He spun the PRV in a half circle and then patted the back. "Hop on."

"How do I get myself into these things," she muttered under her breath. Grasping the safety bar, Millie backed down the ladder and took a tentative step onto the sideboard.

With a foot planted on each side, she gingerly perched on the back corner and then scooched forward until she reached the seat. All the while, Annette held her phone up, a wide smile on her face.

"Someone call up to the bridge so the captain can watch!" Sharky yelled.

"Already done." Donovan waved his radio in the air. "He's on the outboard bridge wing watching."

"Watching me humiliate myself." Millie shaded her eyes. A crowd had gathered along the bridge's railing. Nic, along with several of the ship's officers, stood watching. "Great. We have an audience."

"This is exciting." Sharky rubbed his hands together. "Just think, Millie. We're entertaining not only the passengers, but the crew too."

"I like entertaining people, but not like this." Millie placed both arms around Sharky's waist. "Let's make this a slow and easy ride, do a couple of circles and then take me back to home port."

"You mean like this?" Sharky squeezed the throttle, catapulting the PRV across the open water and flinging her backward. "Hang on."

"Now you tell me." Millie tightened her grip. She gritted her teeth as Sharky swung them around in a tight circle.

Eyeing the wave he had just created, he let out a whoop of joy as they rode the crest, becoming airborne for a moment before landing on the other side.

"Isn't this a blast?" Sharky shouted.

"No, it's terrifying. You're supposed to be part of a rescue team, not a crisis creator."

"Right. You're right. We need to create a staged emergency." Sharky let off the throttle. "Fall in the water so I can rescue you."

"Fall in the water," Millie repeated.

"You know. Up and over." Sharky made a diving motion.

"You want me in the water."

Sharky shifted. "How can I rescue you if you're on the back of the PRV?"

Millie's eyes slid in the direction of the ship, slowly lifting her gaze. Passengers and crewmembers lined the railing. Several waved, and she reluctantly waved back.

Although the bridge was a good distance away, she didn't have to see Nic's face to know he was enjoying the show.

Sharky noticed too. "We gotta prove the PRV is a worthwhile investment. Heave ho." He gave Millie a firm shove, pushing her off the back and into the ocean.

Chapter 7

Millie hit the water face first, almost instantaneously resurfacing in her overinflated lifejacket. "Sharky Kiveski," she sputtered. "What did you do that for?"

"I need to rescue you. Start flailing around in the water, like you're drowning or something. Maybe even pretend a shark is circling you."

"A shark?" Millie spun in a circle, her eyes frantically scanning the deep water.

"Hang tight. Start acting like you're in imminent danger, try screaming or getting my attention, like this is for real." Sharky eased the throttle down, coasting a safe distance away before nailing it. He headed toward the floating ramp, leaving Millie alone in the vast ocean.

She frantically waved her arms. "Sharky! This isn't funny! Come back and get me right now!" Millie kept one eye on the water and the other on the ship. The waves seemed as if they were building, swiftly carrying her even farther away from Siren of the Seas. Either the ship was drifting, or she was, or maybe it was a little of both.

Sharky hit the gas and sped across the open water at a rapid rate. He drew closer, creating a wall of towering waves.

Millie squeezed her eyes shut as she turned her head to avoid a direct hit. "Hurry," she sputtered. "I'm taking in water."

"I'm workin' on it. I'm mapping out my strategy." Sharky and the PRV circled her. "Pretend you're injured."

"Why don't *you* pretend you're injured, because if you don't get me out of this water pronto, I'm going to hurt you."

"Testy, testy. If you didn't want to volunteer, you should've said something."

"Said something?" Millie shrieked. Remembering they had a rather large audience, she lowered her voice. "I told you to pick someone else, but no...you had to pick me."

"Let's not forget how important this drill is." Sharky slowly circled Millie a second time. "What we're doing right now has the potential to save someone's life."

"I get it. I'm trying to do my part but you're making it nearly impossible."

"I have an idea. Flip onto your stomach and do the dead man's float."

"I'm not good at holding my breath."

"This won't take long. I promise, I won't let you drown."

"Fine. Make it quick." Millie flipped over so that she was face down, her arms and legs extended.

Sharky unclipped a bright orange rescue board from the side of the watercraft. Swinging his leg over the seat, he knelt on the footrest before grabbing Millie's lifejacket and flipping her back over. "Hold still."

"I am," she gritted out. "It's the ocean that's moving."

"Okay. Okay. Let's just calm down. We're both new at this rescue thing. There's always a learning curve." He pulled her close and eased the rescue board under her. "We're doing good. Hang in there."

"I'm hanging."

Sharky unstrapped a bungee cord attached to the side of the PRV and then wrapped it around her before securing it.

"What are you doing?"

"Securing you to the rescue board so I can pull you to safety."

Millie's head shot up. "You're towing me back to the boat?"

"Yeah," Sharky snickered. "That's an excellent analogy. I'm towing you to safety."

"Great. Remember, you need to take it slow and easy." Millie gripped the sides of the rescue board, watching as Sharky resumed his position at the helm of the PRV. "Ready?"

"As I'll ever be." Millie clenched the sides of the board, bracing herself as they skimmed over the waves. They drew closer to the ship, and Millie could hear the crowd cheering.

Sharky, reveling in the attention, did a victory lap, waving to the crowds as Millie squeezed her eyes shut. "You got your moment of fame. I'm water-logged and the motion of the ocean is making me nauseous."

"Party pooper." Sharky executed a final turn and dragged Millie alongside the inflatable ramp before slowly climbing it.

She hit the base with a small *thud* before she and the board were being pulled up and onto the deck.

"Well done, Millie." Donovan clapped his hands. "It was a superb performance, a flawlessly executed rescue mission."

Sharky hopped off the PRV and unhooked Millie from the rescue board. "Millie did a great job. She got a little testy at one point but came through like a real trooper in the end."

"Because you left me in the middle of the ocean, bobbing in the water and floundering like a fish."

Sharky gave her a hand up. "Don't be so dramatic. You knew I was coming back for you."

"You both did an outstanding job." Donovan gave Sharky a hearty whack on the back. "Now, if you can do that under extreme duress and in the dark, I think corporate will easily approve of PRV purchases for the rest of the fleet."

Annette hurried over. "I got some amazing video footage."

"Goody." Millie hung the lifejacket on the PRV handle and then unzipped the wetsuit before peeling it off. She ran a light hand over her arms. "The wetsuit is a keeper. I'm dry except for my face, feet and hands."

"And the suit is also insulated," Donovan said.

"I need to get back to work." Several of the crewmembers high-fived Millie on her way past. Now that it was over, she grudgingly admitted it hadn't been horrible.

If taking part in a rescue drill could help save a life or lives, Millie was all for it. And Sharky had been careful transporting her back to the ship, which was important in the event whoever was being rescued might also be injured.

The new PRV would eliminate the crew having to spend precious minutes unloading a lifeboat, not to mention the rescuer would be at water level, giving them a better visual of what was happening.

Danielle and Annette caught up with Millie on her way out. "That looked like a blast," Danielle said.

· "It was exciting. Being out there in the middle of the ocean by myself was a little spooky." Millie couldn't imagine what it would be like to survive going over the side of the ship, only to come to the horrifying realization it was possible that no one knew you had gone over, and you ended up being left behind.

She'd heard of that happening, where someone was caught on camera or visually seen going over the side. By the time the vessel could stop, turn around and go back, it was nearly impossible for the rescue crew, even using large spotlights, to find the person who went overboard. It was a cruise ship's worst nightmare—that and fire.

"So, what's on your schedule for the rest of the day?" Danielle asked.

Millie tapped the top of her scheduler app. "I have a Mix and Mingle Singles party coming up."

"Me too." Danielle leaned in. "We're co-hosting. Andy must be expecting a large crowd. How about you handle the hosting and I'll assist?"

"Are you sure? I know how much you enjoy hosting the mix and mingles," Millie teased.

Danielle curled her lip. "I think Andy gives me those because he knows how much I can't stand them. Speaking of singles mixing and mingling, I ran into Thomas Windsor earlier today."

Millie remembered the brawl between a couple of women during the voyage over, how they went after each other, and Thomas got caught in the middle. "He attends those parties. I'm sure he'll liven things up."

"Without a doubt."

They parted ways in the stairwell, with Millie hosting the Stormy Seas Sailboat contest, where participants tossed miniature sailboats into a life preserver, a fitting game after Sharky and Millie's practice rescue. The game finished, and it was time to head to the single's get-together.

Several attendees were already waiting by the door when Millie arrived to unlock it. A handful of servers buzzed back and forth, setting up for the event.

The lounge quickly filled, and she spotted Thomas off in the corner, surrounded by a group of women.

Kate and Harry Moxey, a couple who were traveling with the Ponsfords and others in Clarissa Sinclair's group, were also attending.

"Hey."

Millie turned to find Danielle standing behind her. "We have quite a turnout."

"No kidding. It's a full house." Millie reached behind the counter and handed Danielle a roll of toilet paper. She briefly explained how her icebreaker game worked. "I'll ask passengers to form groups of six. You take one side of the room while I take the other."

"I think I've heard of this game," Danielle said. "The person has to share things about themselves based on the number of sheets they take. For example, a player who only takes one sheet only has to share one thing while someone who takes six, has to share six things about themselves."

"You got it." Millie addressed the crowd and waited for them to form groups. Danielle took the right-hand side of the room while Millie headed left. She played the game with the first group and then told them they were welcome to order a complimentary drink at the bar for participating.

Kate and Harry Moxey were part of the second group Millie joined. "Welcome to our Mix and Mingle Singles party," she hinted.

"Thank you," Kate beamed. "We love these parties and meet some of the most interesting people."

Harry placed a light hand on his wife's arm. "We thought we might find a few new friends interested in coming to our suite for cocktails later."

"I'm sure you'll have some takers." Millie briefly explained the game before handing the roll of toilet paper to Kate. She stayed long enough to get the "roll rolling."

An attendee pulled her aside, inquiring about the next single's get-together while Danielle headed to the bar to chat with a woman who was alone and looking glum.

Millie caught Thomas's eye and made her way over. "Are you enjoying the cruise so far?" she asked.

"It's wonderful. Just as delightful as the journey over to the UK."

"We're trying to talk Thomas into staying in Florida for a few days after the ship docks," one woman said. "We've been invited to a small party at a friend's condo near South Beach. It should be fun."

"I haven't decided yet," Thomas said. "I'm looking forward to heading home."

"I, for one, am glad to have left Southampton," the woman standing next to Millie said. "The Southampton Strangler struck the other night at a park near the port. It was a little too close for comfort if you ask me."

"Socialite turned reporter, Clarissa Sinclair, no less. I have a friend who is with the police force. Apparently, Clarissa contacted her boss at the news agency hours before her death, claiming she had an inside scoop on the strangler."

Millie's heart skipped a beat. "Did she tell her boss what she'd found?"

"No. Clarissa wouldn't spill the beans. She was much too smart to give away a juicy story about the strangler." The woman lowered her voice. "Of course, the authorities aren't divulging that information since they're investigating."

Millie's mind whirled. What if Sinclair had stumbled upon the strangler's identity? She shot Thomas a furtive glance. His expression mirrored her own—shock at the revelation. Or was it an act?

Surely, the authorities were retracing Clarissa's steps, talking to anyone she'd been with, or around, leading up to that fateful night. Prime suspects would not only be the Moxeys, but the Ponsfords and Bruce and Hilda Ellis, not to mention Thomas. How well had he known Clarissa?

Millie, pouncing on the perfect opening, turned to Thomas. "Did you know Clarissa?"

"In passing. She was friends of my traveling companions, an acquaintance in a roundabout way." Thomas told them he'd stayed at a hotel down the street while Clarissa and the other couples all stayed in the same hotel. His watch chimed. "Time for dinner." He excused himself and left Millie and the two women behind.

"Thank you for hosting such a fun event."

"You're welcome. I'm glad you enjoyed it. There will be many more during our voyage." Millie, along with Danielle, stayed behind to help the servers clean up.

The evening's activities were in full swing, and Millie began making her way through her evening schedule, from helping the ship's dancers through several outfit changes to the Piano Bar and then to the other side of the ship.

Ocean Treasures big event—the gold-by-the-inch sale—was in full swing, and it was wall-to-wall shoppers. The crowd forced Millie to backtrack and find another route down to the comedy club, where she caught a few minutes of Donovan's new show.

As the evening wore on, Millie's steps dragged. It had been a full day of non-stop activities, something she was no longer accustomed to since the British Isles had been port-intensive. It would take a few more sea days for her to get back into the groove of the added activities and events.

Her scheduler app chimed, reminding her to pop into her last event when her radio went off. "Alpha! Alpha! Alpha!"

Chapter 8

Millie recognized Oscar's voice as he barked the emergency code, followed by the location—deck three, and not far from the photo gallery, which had long since closed for the day.

She hustled down the stairs, making it in record time. Millie bypassed the passengers' cabins. Mere steps from the photo gallery, she found a small group of the ship's personnel gathered around someone who was sprawled out on the floor.

As she drew closer, Millie realized it was Hilda Ellis.

"It's my ankle," Hilda winced. "I'm telling you, someone was following me."

"I'm sorry, Mrs. Ellis. We've searched the area. The person you're describing is no longer around,"

Oscar said. "Please explain again, to our ship's head of security, exactly what happened."

Hilda explained that she'd decided to go up to the lido deck to grab some hot tea. "The ship is really rocking. It was making me nauseous, so I thought tea might settle my stomach before bed. That's when I noticed I was being followed."

Patterson interrupted. "But you never saw anyone?"

"No. It was just a feeling. You know, when your scalp tingles and you're certain someone is nearby."

Patterson and Oscar exchanged a quick glance.

"You don't believe me."

"Please. Go on," Patterson said.

"I heard a muffled slam, so I hurried to the stairwell, which is when I tripped over your potted palm tree. It's a horrid spot for a fake plant, not to mention it's in desperate need of a good dusting."

"The ship's medical staff has arrived with a wheelchair. You'll be taken down to our center for a thorough examination."

"I'm sure I just twisted my ankle when I fell." Hilda continued talking as the ship's medical staff helped her into the wheelchair. "I'm telling you...someone was following me."

"I'll add some extra patrols to this area," Patterson promised. "In the meantime, if you're concerned about your safety, I suggest you avoid venturing off on your own, particularly after dark and late at night. Are you traveling by yourself?"

"I'm on board with my husband. He's in the casino. I don't want to bother him. It was a minor slip. Besides, he'll be miffed if I pull him away from his poker game especially if he has a hot hand."

"I'll join Mrs. Ellis in the medical center and then accompany her back to her cabin," Millie offered.

Patterson shifted to the side. "I would appreciate that."

Millie nodded to the medical staff. "I'll be along shortly." She waited for them to wheel the woman into the nearby elevator and for the doors to close. "A word of warning. I've had a few, shall we say, encounters with Mrs. Ellis. You need to handle her with a large dose of patience."

"What's your take on her claim she's being followed?" Patterson asked. "Oscar wasn't far away and was the first on scene. He said there was no one around."

"I can't vouch for whether she has a penchant for exaggerating." Millie had another thought. "You don't think she staged an injury to sue the cruise line for a slip and fall, do you?"

Patterson rubbed his chin. "We've had our share of those. It's hard to tell."

Oscar, who had remained silent, spoke. "She was very distraught and trembling when I arrived. I believe she thought someone was following her."

"I had better head down to medical." Millie turned to go. "Is there any recent news about the strangler?"

"Not yet."

"I spoke with a passenger earlier, whose friend is a member of the police force. According to what she was told, Clarissa contacted her boss at the news agency hours before her death, claiming she had an inside scoop on the strangler. I've been giving it some thought."

"And?" Patterson prompted.

"A handful of our passengers traveled to Southampton on our original voyage, which makes them even greater persons of interest. The strangler picked up again, shortly after our arrival and then the last victim was murdered only steps away from where our ship docked. My guess is it's more than a coincidence." Millie shifted her feet. "Why wouldn't the authorities detain these passengers, perhaps even prevent them from boarding the ship?"

"No probable cause. Suspicion? Certainly, but you can't hold people on a hunch," Patterson said. "Besides, we're keeping tabs on them the best that we can, given the fact that they're on a ship with thousands of other passengers."

A troubling thought crossed Millie's mind. "If the strangler's victims were specific targets in the UK, then it's possible there won't be any further incidents. He...or she...finished what they set out to do and are now cruising back to the States."

Patterson gave Millie a grim smile. "The good guys don't always get the bad guys. If what you theorize is true, then another bad guy—a serial killer at that—will be walking the streets, sipping piña coladas, living among us, possibly even right under our noses."

During her trek to the medical center, Millie ticked off the list of potential suspects. Certainly, everyone in Sinclair's party had the opportunity, but what was the motive?

Unless, as she'd heard, the woman had inadvertently stumbled upon the strangler's identity. The strangler found out and killed her. But why dump her body near the port? Wouldn't the killer want the body somewhere else...to lead authorities away from the ship?

After first hearing about the Southampton Strangler, Millie had done some research and discovered serial killers possessed similar traits. They were smooth talkers with illusions of grandiosity. They got their kicks from taunting the police, a sort of cat-and-mouse game, getting thrills from the chase and staying one step ahead.

If that were true, and the killer was on board the ship, it would be the perfect setup for "getting away" with the murder, frustrating the local authorities and cleverly believing they were untouchable in another country.

If she really thought about it, having the strangler leaving his last victim a stone's throw away from the port, only hours before stepping on board the ship and getting away scot-free with a recent round of killings, would fit their MO.

She reached the medical center and stepped inside the empty waiting area. Millie could hear echoes of voices coming from the back. Hilda's unmistakable voice was part of the mix.

Moments later, the door separating the waiting area from the examining rooms flew open and a red-faced Hilda limped out. Doctor Gundervan and Gavin Framm, the ship's head nurse, followed close behind.

"I don't need a wheelchair. I'll take it easy but feel I can control my health better than you and your staff. Your x-ray equipment is rudimentary. I'm sure I pulled a muscle when I fell."

"I would like you to stop by tomorrow for another checkup," the doctor said, "to ensure we didn't miss anything in the first set of x-rays.

Unless, of course, you'll let me take the last few now."

"I'm tired of being poked and prodded," she grumbled. "I'm exhausted. It's past my bedtime and I'm getting cranky because I'm hungry."

"Very well, then. I can't keep you here against your will." The doctor looked relieved to see Millie. "Millie will accompany you back to your cabin. Call me tomorrow when you're ready to come down for a follow-up visit."

"We'll see about that." Hilda sniffled loudly. "I'll see how I feel in the morning."

Millie offered the woman a cautious smile as she held the door. "Have you talked to your husband? Does he know you're down here?"

"No. Like I said earlier, he's in the casino and will be there until they close for the night. He doesn't like me bothering him when he's playing. It messes up his concentration."

Millie didn't doubt that for a second. The woman was, at best, trying, and not a particularly positive force. "You said you were hungry. Would you like me to place an order for room service?"

"No thanks. I've already checked out the menu. Stale club sandwiches and cold fries don't sound appealing." Hilda brightened. "It's Mexican buffet night. I wouldn't mind running up there to grab a bite to eat."

Millie hadn't eaten either. Since she'd promised Patterson that she would escort the injured woman to her cabin, she offered to accompany her to the buffet.

"Do you like Mexican food?" Hilda asked.

"Yes, but sometimes it doesn't like me."

"Me either, but I love it." Hilda smacked her lips.

It was a slow go, and several times Millie offered to get a wheelchair, but Hilda refused.

Finally, the women reached the buffet. The place was packed, but it didn't deter Hilda. She cut to the front of the line, complaining loudly that she was injured. She placed a dinnerplate on her tray before making her way along the serving stations.

She loaded it with one of everything...a chicken enchilada, a wet burrito, beef tostada, a shrimp quesadilla, and a trio of hard tacos. Her plate was full, but Hilda somehow managed to add a heaping mound of refried beans smack dab in the center.

It was late, and the last thing Millie wanted to do was go to bed on a full stomach, so she fixed two crunchy tacos, light on the meat and heavy on the lettuce and tomato, before joining Hilda at a handicapped table nearby. "Can I get you a drink? Perhaps the tea you mentioned earlier?"

"That would be nice. Bring a cup of hot water and a tea bag. I'll fix it myself. I don't like it too strong. It leaves a bitter taste in my mouth."

"Of course." Millie made her way to the beverage station. She filled a glass with ice and water before filling Hilda's cup with hot water. She tucked a tea bag in her pocket and carried both back to their table.

"Thank you." Hilda winced slightly as she shifted her ample frame.

"Is your ankle still bothering you?"

"It's my back now, but only when I turn a certain way." Hilda removed the tea bag from the wrapper and dunked it in her cup. "I'm sure your bosses think I'm going to sue for my injury, but I'm not."

"We don't want to see anyone injured, and I'm certain the potted palm has found a new home by now."

"Hopefully, they blew off some of the dust while they were at it."

Millie changed the subject. "I'm sorry to hear about the death of your friend, Ms. Sinclair."

"Clarissa?" Hilda perused her plate and then methodically began sampling a bite of everything.

"We used to be a lot closer. She changed the last few years. The whole reporter thing went right to her head, not to mention she tried to fit into the socialite scene. She got a little too rich for my blood."

"So, you weren't close friends."

"Not anymore." Hilda grew quiet as she polished off the tacos and then began sipping her tea. "Her husband, Norbert, left her a rather large amount of life insurance money. She changed after that."

"But she decided to cruise to the States with your group," Millie prompted. "Which means she wasn't planning on working."

"Clarissa only did the reporter thing for attention. She loved the spotlight, loved being the center of attention." Hilda's expression grew thoughtful. "Her goal in life was to be rich and famous. In a way, she managed to accomplish both."

"Did she mention if she'd been following the case of the Southampton Strangler?"

"Nope. In fact, I had no idea she was even investigating until I heard something about it on the news this evening. Clarissa could be tight-lipped if she needed to."

"Her holiday home, was it near yours?"

"No. Hers was in a gated community. When you're a socialite at her level of standing, you can't live among the commoners."

Millie detected a hint of bitterness in Hilda's voice.

"Money has a way of changing people."

"It certainly does." Hilda folded her quesadilla in half and savored her first bite. "This is delicious," she mumbled. "It's even better than the tacos."

"It looks tasty."

Hilda eyed Millie's nearly empty plate. "That's all you're eating?"

"I have a hard time sleeping if I eat too much before going to bed."

"I've never had that problem. The fuller the better is my motto," Hilda said. "I think there was one more reason Clarissa was keen on joining us for the cruise."

"Which was?" Millie prompted.

"I think she had a crush on Edward and Annabel's friend, Thomas Windsor. Maybe he was somehow involved in her death."

Chapter 9

"You...you think that Clarissa had a crush on Thomas Windsor?" Millie stammered. "I wonder if the investigators know that."

Hilda grabbed a tortilla chip and dipped it in her salsa. "I told them all about it. I don't mean to be rude, but I need to finish eating before my food gets cold."

While Hilda ate, Millie thought about what she'd said. Thomas Windsor was dashing and sophisticated, emanating an aura of mystery and charm. Women swooned over him. It was easy to understand why Clarissa was no different. He had women chasing him around all the time and could easily handle an "overly eager" admirer.

Besides, what reason would he have to kill Clarissa? Unless Clarissa had uncovered something about Thomas. Perhaps she suspected him of being the strangler and contacted her office to let them know she had a story.

What if he had found out and somehow lured her to a remote area of the park where he strangled her? But if Hilda had told the authorities what she knew, then why would they allow him to leave the country?

Surely, they could've come up with some minor offense to detain him and prevent him from boarding Siren of the Seas.

Although it was circumstantial. Yes, Thomas may have had the opportunity *and* motive *if* he was the strangler. It was a huge *IF*.

"How well do you know the Moxeys?"

"We all used to hang around in the same group together until Kate and Harry decided to spice up their marriage."

"Spice up their marriage?" Millie echoed.

"You'll find out soon enough if you spend time around them." Hilda burped. "Excuse me." She scraped the sauce off the bottom of her now empty plate. "Edward...Eddie and Annabel are great. We've been friends with them for almost as long as Clarissa and Norbert before his death." Hilda downed the last of her tea. "You seem quite interested in my friends and the strangler."

"I'm just curious about the case."

Hilda scooched out of her chair. "I like to believe I'm smarter than the average person. If you ask me, I think the strangler finished what he set out to do and now he'll go dormant again."

While they walked, Hilda bombarded Millie with questions about the ship, about security and crewmembers' private quarters, and then began offering unsolicited advice on what she thought should be added in the way of entertainment.

By the time they reached the woman's cabin, Millie's ears were ringing, and she felt copious amounts of compassion for her husband, Bruce.

Hilda slipped her keycard in the slot, eased the door open and switched the lights on.

From Millie's hallway vantage point, she could see the compact cabin was empty. "Your husband is still in the casino?"

"He'll be there until they close. Hopefully, he's up. He lost some money last night." Hilda thanked her for accompanying her back to the cabin and, after she left, Millie got the impression the woman was lonely. Bruce may or may not be a big gambler, but she secretly suspected the casino was his escape.

She finished her last rounds and returned to the apartment. Nic, who had been on the bridge, was close behind. "That was a rough one."

"Without a doubt."

Nic removed his jacket and gave her a quick hug. "It was a long day."

"Extremely, like squeezing two days of events into one. These long sea days are going to take some getting used to."

"Here. Here." Nic followed Scout and Millie onto the balcony.

The night skies were clear and filled with a dazzling array of twinkling stars. "It's beautiful. You may have missed it, but we had red skies at night."

"Sailor's delight. Meaning we're in store for some pleasant weather." Millie squeezed in closer, and Nic wrapped his arms around her.

"I thoroughly enjoyed your rescue mission."

"Ugh." Millie groaned. "Sharky put us through the paces."

"You handled it like a real team player."

"Thanks."

"I heard we had a little excitement with one of the passengers."

"Hilda Ellis. She thought someone was following her, wasn't watching where she was going and collided with a potted palm. I joined her for a late dinner and then accompanied her back to her cabin."

"From what I'm being told, some passengers are jittery. I believe the rumor about the strangler being on board the ship is making its rounds."

"Rumor," Millie echoed. "So, there's no proof yet that he or she boarded the ship?"

"No. What we know is we need to be on guard, passengers and crew alike. The security department is issuing a reminder about passenger's safety. I'm not sure if it's gone out yet."

The couple chatted about the next day's schedule and then turned in. Exhausted, Millie fell asleep as soon as her head hit the pillow. She didn't stir until the alarm clock woke her early the next morning.

Repeating her previous day, Millie joined Annette for several brisk strolls around the jogging track. While they walked, she filled her friend in on all that had transpired the previous night.

"I guess it's best for us to be on guard," Annette said. "I'll call a meeting this morning, not to scare my staff but to make them more aware."

"Especially those who deliver room service." Millie's morning flew by. During her lunchbreak, she headed down to the crew's dining room.

Danielle arrived midway through the meal and joined her.

"How's your day?"

"Crazy. Andy has me running all over the ship. Scavenger hunts, co-hosting the art auction. CHOG duty is up next."

CHOGS was the crewmember's nickname for chair hogs, passengers who got up early in the morning and headed down to the pool area to save primo seats by placing their belongings on them. Later in the morning, they would show up to claim their spots. Many were repeat offenders.

It hadn't been an issue during the British Isles' summer months, but now that they were returning to balmier weather, Siren of the Seas had once again begun cracking down on the CHOGS.

"I'm on break for a few. Would you like some help?"

"Yeah, I can always use some backup."

"I'm your gal." After finishing and on their way upstairs, Millie filled Danielle in on Hilda's accident and their conversation during dinner.

"Wow. So, Thomas Windsor might be the Southampton Strangler."

"Or someone in their party. If you base it strictly on clues, Thomas makes the most sense."

"He seems like such a nice guy," Danielle said.

"Some notorious serial killers were nice guys; people you would never suspect."

They reached the lido deck and headed to the main pool—the largest and busiest. The first two rows of loungers were either occupied or had items placed on the seats.

Millie headed in the opposite direction of Danielle, collecting beach bags and towels, along with paperback and hardcover books. She turned them over to the crewmember who was working at the towel station.

She began a second round of pickups when she noticed Danielle chatting with a young passenger. Millie could see the boy was visibly upset as she dropped off the collected items and made her way over. "What's going on?"

"I need to have my mother's stuff left on this chair," the boy said. "Mummy wants this chair."

"Where is Mummy?" Millie glanced around.

"In our cabin."

"Did she leave for a moment to go pick something up?"

The boy lowered his gaze.

"Let me guess. She's sleeping."

"She'll be up any minute now, and she's going to be furious with me if she doesn't get this chair."

"I see." Millie dug into her pocket and grabbed her notepad and pen. She jotted down a quick note. "Please take this to your mother and let her know chair saving is not allowed."

The boy's eyes grew round as saucers. "She's going to be angry."

"Then please tell her to contact the guest services desk so they can explain the policy to her."

"Okay."

Millie's heart went out to the boy as she watched him walk off with his mother's bag. "I like to think of this as an exercise in passenger retraining. I'm hoping once they realize we mean business, it will become less of a problem."

"It might take some time." Danielle thanked her for the backup and then Millie headed to her next event. It was early afternoon before her next break. She made a beeline for Patterson's office to share what she'd heard from Hilda Ellis the previous evening.

His door was ajar, and she could hear voices coming from within. Millie gave it a light rap and then stuck her head inside.

Patterson was there, along with Nic and a somber Donovan Sweeney. "I'm sorry. I didn't mean to interrupt." She started to back out when she noticed another person, this one seated in front of the desk, and a portable fingerprinting machine in front of him.

Chapter 10

Millie's eyes flitted from Andy, who was seated in front of the fingerprinting machine, to Dave Patterson. "At the risk of sounding nosy, what's going on?"

"The authorities have requested Andy to submit a set of fingerprints for their investigation into Clarissa Sinclair's murder."

"They can't seriously suspect Andy."

"They caught me on surveillance camera in the area a short time before the woman's body was found. I suppose it doesn't help that I'm British, and Siren of the Seas began its summer itinerary when the first in the new round of killings took place."

"We're hoping it's merely a formality," Donovan said. "They'll get Andy's prints, clear his name and then remove him from the list of suspects."

Millie thought about Hilda Ellis's claim someone was following her. "Were you able to check the ship's cameras to find out if Hilda's insistence she was being followed last night panned out?"

"We did." Patterson told her they'd gone over the surveillance and found the clip of Ellis. "She appeared nervous and was looking over her shoulder, which was when she tripped over the potted palm. Unfortunately, no one else was caught on camera or found in the vicinity."

"Either she was mistaken or whoever was following her was aware of the cameras and avoided them." Millie had another thought. "If the authorities are asking for a print, they must've found something at the scene."

"They're not sharing as much information as I had hoped." Frustrated, Patterson tossed his pen on the desk and leaned back in his chair. "All I know is if I were going to murder Clarissa Sinclair, I certainly wouldn't want to be a part of the group she was traveling with."

"Unless, as I mentioned last night, she had a hot lead on the strangler and planned to reveal his identity, forcing his or her hand."

"A valid point. The killer is clever and has eluded the authorities for years now. They may have gotten a little careless in their haste to take the woman out."

"I'm guessing the authorities would want the fingerprints of the other suspects."

"I'm sure they already have them," Nic said.

"So, none of them are a match." Millie began pacing. "Unless the print they found doesn't belong to any of them or the strangler."

"I'm sure you didn't randomly drop by," Patterson said. "Is there something you needed?"

"I had a long conversation with Hilda last night before I escorted her to her cabin." Millie told them what the woman had said, how Clarissa had shown an interest in Thomas Windsor.

"He's on the radar."

"I was thinking, if the authorities could retrace Sinclair's steps prior to her murder, they might be able to figure out who she was with and what she may have found."

Donovan wagged his finger. "I recognize the look in your eyes, Millie. You should leave well enough alone."

"Did I say I was planning on investigating?" Millie feigned innocence. "I don't see the harm in doing a little online research to possibly pick up on something others may have missed."

Patterson opened his mouth to reply, and Nic lifted a hand, cutting him off. "You know my wife well enough by now. She isn't going to keep her nose out of it."

Millie lifted her chin. "I'm trying to help."

"I know your intentions are well-meaning," Nic said. "Let me rephrase that. My wife is going to poke around in the case whether we like it or not."

"That sounds better. Carry on." Millie squared her shoulders and marched out of Patterson's office. Admittedly, it probably wasn't her concern, but there was no harm in doing a little digging around on her own.

But first, Millie needed to head upstairs to host "Dress the Guest," a timed game where teams dressed a "teammate" using only one hand.

Over the past several months, the entertainment department had accumulated boxes of clothing donated by crewmembers, as well as clothing and accessories that were left behind by passengers and never claimed.

Today she was "upping the game" by including some interesting items borrowed from the excursions desk.

Millie, along with her co-host, Kevin, assembled several teams before handing out the items. There were bathing suits, yoga pants, tank tops, flip-flops, ball caps, and an array of accessories. Millie passed out the first round of items before getting to the good stuff.

She grabbed the box of goodies Isla had loaned her, and a collective moan went up as she handed out dive masks, snorkels, and fins.

A crowd gathered, watching as the participants struggled to dress their teammate. When the time was up, Millie blew her whistle, and they began removing the items, counting as they went. The onlookers applauded as she passed out complimentary mini-manicures or pedicures to the winners, and then she and Kevin made quick work of putting everything away.

During her afternoon break, she headed home and let Scout onto the balcony. She finished fixing a sandwich and settled in at the desk.

Yip. Millie heard a small whine and felt a gentle tug on her pant leg. Scout stood staring at her. "I suppose you think you need to be in my lap."

She scooped him up and held him close. His nose twitched as he zeroed in on her food. "Yes, you can have some." Millie tore off a small piece of meat and fed it to him before shifting her attention to the computer.

In between bites, she sorted through her emails. After finishing, she opened a new search screen and typed in "Southampton Strangler." A screen full of stories popped up. Millie clicked through the first few and quickly realized they all said the same thing. The strangler had been quiet for five years and then, out-of-the-blue, started killing again.

She grabbed a sheet of paper and began jotting down some notes.

The first victim was Edith Branson, a sixty-four-year-old woman who lived in an upscale North Southampton neighborhood. According to the story, Edith had contacted the local authorities

148

after spotting a strange man lurking in her gardens. Edith had also survived the strangler's attack back in 2015.

The second victim was a uni student. The story suggested the authorities believed the strangler took her charm bracelet as a souvenir.

Millie remembered hearing about the third. It was a woman who lived in nearby Midanbury. She left home to walk her dog around dusk and never returned. They found her body in a nearby park and her poor pup was guarding it. One bright blue training shoe was missing and believed to have been taken by the strangler.

The most recent victim was reporter and socialite Clarissa Sinclair. There was no mention of any missing items but, similar to what Halbert had said, Clarissa had put up a fight and the authorities believed she'd injured her attacker.

Four women with no direct link between the victims. In fact, Millie wondered if perhaps Clarissa was never intended to be a victim, but had

149

inadvertently placed herself on the strangler's radar while snooping around and possibly uncovering his or her identity.

Millie shoved the chair back and carried Scout to the balcony. It was no surprise Edith Branson would be a target, particularly since she'd survived a previous attack.

The uni student and jogger were a mystery. Why them? There had to be a motive. Or did there? Millie knew that serial killers were also known to have randomly selected their victims, which was why the authorities had a tough time tracking them down.

She thought about Thomas Windsor and what Hilda had said. Was Clarissa interested in Thomas? Had she inadvertently found something out about him, jokingly mentioned it to him, and he took her out?

Perhaps he felt his back was against the wall. If Thomas was the strangler and had killed Clarissa, he may have taken a gamble and murdered her, knowing he was only hours away from leaving the country.

She returned to her desk and logged onto the ship's computer system. She pulled up the manifest and typed Thomas's name in the search bar. His date of birth was listed as January 1, 1956. His address was listed as Lexington, Kentucky.

Millie clicked out of the ship's database and opened a new screen. She typed his name and location into the search bar. An older story popped up, one she vaguely remembered reading about some time ago, when an unrelated and tragic death occurred on board the ship and she suspected Thomas might be involved.

She reread the story about how Thomas's wife, Elizabeth, had died of a single, self-inflicted gunshot wound. Thomas claimed he had spent the night in the horse barn, waiting for the birth of a foal, and had slept on a cot in the tack room. It wasn't until early the next morning when he returned to the main house to shower and check on

Elizabeth that he found her dead on the bedroom floor.

The story explained that Elizabeth, whose family had founded an equestrian center, along with a museum and educational theme park, had complained of debilitating joint pain and body aches for months. Despite running exhaustive tests, doctors could find no reason for her pain.

The authorities detained Thomas, questioning him at length. He'd even agreed to take a polygraph test. The results of the test were inconclusive. With no evidence linking Thomas to his wife's death, it was ruled a suicide, and the case was closed.

Elizabeth's brother was also interviewed. He accused Thomas of keeping Elizabeth from her family and insisted he was responsible for his sister's death.

Had Thomas murdered his wife? Perhaps she knew he was the strangler, and he killed her.

Millie was determined to delve into Clarissa's final hours and vowed to speak to the people who could help fill in the blanks, but it would have to wait. She needed to get back to work.

The hours flew by as Millie moved from event to event. She hosted an afternoon tea and was thrilled to discover Kate Moxey and Annabel Ponsford were there, giving her the perfect opportunity to question Clarissa's friends.

She waited until the end of the event to approach their table. They made small talk and then Millie got right to the point, asking if they had been updated on Clarissa's investigation.

"The authorities have questioned all of us at length," Annabel said. "I think Clarissa, bless her heart, was a bit of a snoop, suspected the strangler's identity and maybe even confronted the individual."

Kate nodded in agreement. "Clarissa was chuffed about her reporter job and it made her cheeky."

"Chuffed? Cheeky?" Millie asked.

"Chuffed means to be pleased," Annabel explained. "And cheeky is having the last word or knowing everything."

"So, she may have gone full blazes and confronted the strangler, not realizing she had written her own death sentence."

"Exactly," Kate said. "We were discussing her death since the authorities are hot on the case."

"Because you might unwittingly have valuable information."

Annabel nibbled her lower lip. "If the authorities think we might have valuable information and the strangler is on board the ship, it means we might be in danger as well."

"I'm certain security is keeping a close eye on you." Millie swiped at a small crumb on the table. "Out of curiosity, did Clarissa do or say anything that might've been a clue?"

The women exchanged a quick glance and then both shook their heads.

"She joined us later in the evening, claiming she had to take care of some pressing issues. Clarissa seemed excited about the voyage. Looking back, perhaps she was sitting on the information about the strangler and was looking forward to spilling the beans." Annabel shifted her gaze, peering over Millie's shoulder. "Our husbands are here. It's time to get going."

"We're heading to the art auction to peruse the new pieces and to sip some champagne." Kate scooted out of the booth as her husband, along with the Ellises and Edward Ponsford, made their way over. "We were discussing poor Clarissa. We heard Millie is somewhat of a super sleuth, at least that's what Thomas told us, so we were sharing information."

"A sleuth," Harry repeated.

"It's a bad habit," Millie said. "My friend, Halbert Pennyman, lives near the scene where the death occurred."

"Are they thinking perhaps the chap might've seen something?" Edward asked.

"I don't know." Millie grew uncomfortable, reminding herself that if the strangler was on board the ship, she might very well be talking to him...her. "I've tried to keep my nose out of this one since I haven't been following the case," she fibbed.

"Best that you do." Edward offered his wife his arm. "We need to head downstairs before they run out of champagne."

Kate arched a brow. "Millie, will you be hosting the Mix and Mingles Singles' party again this evening?"

"No. Not this time."

"It's a shame. Harry and I had such fun at the last event."

"And made some new friends." Harry winked at his wife.

"I'm sure I'll be hosting again soon." Millie thanked the women for the chat and then watched them walk away. If Clarissa's friends and acquaintances knew where she had been or what she'd been doing prior to meeting up with them hours before her death, they weren't talking.

Millie swung by the guest services desk to check with the staff and inquire about comments or complaints regarding the entertainment. Since her friend Nikki was on duty, she waited until she was free before approaching the counter. "I'm here to find out how we're doing."

"I only have one complaint that the passenger asked to be escalated to the captain."

"Let me guess...it's directed at me and from a passenger who is ticked because I removed her items from one of the pool's lounge chairs."

Nikki gave her a thumbs up. "Bingo. At first, I thought you had tossed her stuff over the side of the ship the way she was carrying on."

"Perhaps she should think twice before having her son do her dirty work and save her a primo lounge chair."

"She conveniently left that part out," Nikki said. "As requested, I forwarded her complaint to the captain."

Millie thanked her for the heads up and then took the side stairs to deck seven. She reached the gift shop and caught a glimpse of Cat. She gave her friend a quick wave before making her way inside. "Hey, Millie."

"Hey, Cat. How's business?"

"Busy." Cat tucked a pile of receipts under the cash drawer. "It's been one of those days."

"What's wrong?"

"Andy. He told me Patterson called him down to his office to have him fingerprinted. The UK authorities are taking a closer look at him. Andy is no killer. It's almost laughable except it's not funny."

Millie patted her arm. "I'm sure once they compare his prints to those they have, they'll clear him." She watched as her friend twisted the diamond bracelet Andy had recently surprised Cat with.

The sparkles caught her eye, and then she noticed something else...a small charm. Millie remembered the day Andy had shown it to her, eager to get her opinion before giving it to Cat.

She remembered the trio of small diamonds but didn't remember it having a charm. "I didn't know the bracelet Andy gave you had a charm."

"It didn't." Cat ran her finger over the top. "He picked it up before we left Southampton. He told me he found it at a small jewelry shop close to the port."

Millie thought about another charm bracelet, the one the uni student was wearing when she was strangled.

Chapter 11

Millie's mind whirled. Andy left the ship early the same morning Clarissa's body was found. Andy had a bruise on his head and a scratch on his arm. Siren of the Seas arrived in Southampton only days before the strangler reappeared and murdered his next victim.

"What's wrong?" Cat asked.

"I..." Millie did a mental shake. "Nothing. I just remembered something. I need to run back to the apartment to check on Scout." She hastily said goodbye and then hurried out of the shop.

Back home, Millie made a beeline for the computer and did a quick search for a picture of the charm bracelet the strangler reportedly took. Her heart sank when she discovered the authorities had not only not released a photo, but still hadn't confirmed the bracelet had been taken.

Millie needed to narrow down the list of suspects. Unfortunately, two of her favorite people, Andy and Thomas Windsor, were at the top of the list.

Her last break arrived, and she thought about heading down to the crew dining room but changed her mind and stopped by the galley instead. Millie found her friend in the pantry, taking inventory. "Knock, knock."

Annette pivoted, peering at Millie over the rim of her reading glasses. "Hey, Millie. What's up?"

"Not much. I'm on my dinner break and thought I would stop by to chat and maybe grab one of the RTG meals. You don't have any left."

"I can't keep those in stock. I guess I'm not the only one who wants nutritious meals they can grab and go." Annette placed her clipboard and pen on top of a row of canned vegetables. "What sounds good?"

"Something quick and easy and not a lot of trouble."

"I was thinking about eating, too. Let's see what we can find." Annette, with Millie's help, whipped up a quick meal and then they gathered at the center counter.

After they finished praying, Millie filled her friend in on what she'd learned, how Clarissa may have unwittingly placed herself in a dangerous situation. "I spoke to some of her traveling companions. According to what they told me they have no idea what she was doing in the hours leading up to her death."

"So, Clarissa may have tracked down some clues about the killer, possibly even confronted him or hinted she was onto him and he killed her."

"That's what I think." Millie savored a spoonful of gazpacho, the tangy tomato and garlic tickling her tastebuds. "You make *the* best gazpacho."

"Thanks. It's one of my favorites now that I'm trying to eat healthier."

"How do you think you're doing?"

"I give myself a seven out of ten." Annette tipped her hand. "I still get stressed but then it kinda goes with the territory."

"A seven is fair." Millie finished her soup before reaching for her sandwich. "I'm also thinking either "a," the strangler strategically left Clarissa's body near the port, knowing the authorities might suspect he or she boarded a ship or "b," he didn't plan on killing her and it threw him, or her, off. In other words, the strangler got spooked."

Annette reached for her napkin. "Does it strike you as odd that her traveling companions continued on instead of staying behind?"

"It would, except for the fact Annabel Ponsford told me her in-laws were closer to Clarissa than they were."

"Do you still think it could be Thomas Windsor?"

"Unfortunately, yes. Hilda Ellis told me Clarissa was attracted to Thomas." Millie mentioned her discovery about his wife's suicide. "What if she didn't commit suicide?"

"Correct me if I'm wrong, but didn't the strangler take souvenirs from his victims?" Annette asked.

"At first they said the strangler had, but they've since backtracked and now claim they're not sure. The jogger was missing a blue tennis shoe and the uni student was missing a charm bracelet. I..."

"What?" Annette prompted.

"Nothing." Millie lowered her gaze.

"You were going to say something else. Is there another person you suspect?"

"Yes."

"And..."

"It's Andy," Millie blurted out. "He gave Cat that bracelet. It has diamonds. He recently gave her a charm to add to the bracelet."

"And it matches the description of the bracelet the strangler took from one of his victims?"

"I don't know." Millie, losing her appetite at the thought, pushed her plate away. "The authorities asked Andy to submit a set of fingerprints."

"I'm not surprised, considering he was in the area shortly before her body was found. "Have you asked Andy about it?"

"No. I mean, I feel terrible even putting his name out there."

Annette motioned to what was left of Millie's sandwich. "You gonna eat the rest of your food?"

"No."

Annette polished off Millie's leftovers. "You and I both know Andy didn't kill anyone. If you think this

Thomas Windsor dude is a potential suspect, then find out."

"You mean, sneak into his cabin and look for clues, like a charm bracelet and a blue shoe? Believe me, I've already thought about it."

"So, what's stopping you?"

"I might not like what I find," Millie said miserably. "I don't want it to be Thomas."

"Look at it this way, you would eliminate a suspect."

"True." Millie hopped off the barstool and carried their dirty dishes to the sink. "Thanks for lending an ear."

"You're welcome." Annette trailed behind. "Have you asked Cat what she thinks?"

"No. She's already kinda bummed about it."

"Cat hasn't had much luck with men. I'll never forget how her ex tracked her down and tried to kill her."

"I'm glad he's back in prison where he belongs." Millie rinsed the dishes before placing them in the dishwasher. "I feel somewhat responsible for encouraging her and Andy's relationship."

"Andy's no killer." Annette balled up her napkin and tossed it in the trash. "At least I hope not. That would mean I'm a terrible judge of character."

"Me too." Millie thanked her again and began making her final rounds, starting on the top deck and working her way down. She hovered in the doorway of the comedy club, catching a few lines, and could feel her eyelids drooping.

She did a mental shake and then headed to the nearby side stairwell. It was past midnight, and the shortcut to the upper decks was quiet and empty.

Millie grasped the handrail and began climbing.

Ting.

She paused; certain she'd heard a *tinging* sound.

There was nothing but silence.

Millie kept climbing and reached the next landing.

Tap. Tap. Instead of a *ting*, she could've sworn she heard footsteps.

Millie stopped. The footsteps stopped.

Convinced she was being followed. Millie fumbled for her stun gun, taking the steps two at a time.

Tap. Tap. Tap.

She was in between decks now, and the tapping was growing louder.

Millie raced to the corner and slipped behind a large easel board display of a dark-haired woman in a relaxed pose, her eyes closed with a tranquil ocean as the backdrop.

Her hand trembled as she clutched the stun gun. There was no *ting*, no *tap*. In fact, it was eerily quiet.

All she could hear was her own heart beating loudly. Millie began counting and then eased her way out from behind the sign. *You're getting paranoid, Millie. Just like Hilda Ellis.*

She relaxed her grip on the stun gun and began climbing again.

Tap. Tap. Tap. Tap.

Millie sprinted up the steps as she fumbled with the stun gun's safety switch. She reached the bridge deck and cast a furtive glance behind her.

Not paying attention to where she was going, she tripped on a safety strip, instinctively squeezing the stun gun's trigger as she crashed head-on into someone who was standing on the landing.

Zap.

Chapter 12

An electric jolt shot up Millie's arm, and she simultaneously realized two things: She was still squeezing the stun gun's trigger, and she was zapping her boss.

She immediately released her grip. "Oh, my gosh. Andy."

Andy slumped against the wall, his chest heaving as he struggled to speak.

"I'm sorry. I...I heard someone coming up behind me on the stairwell and I freaked out."

Andy's lip twitched, his breaths coming in quick bursts.

"Do you want me to call medical?"

"No." Andy's head flopped to the side. "Give me a few minutes."

Millie continued rambling and apologizing as she attempted to explain her actions. "Please, God. Don't let Andy die."

"I'm not dying," he gasped. "Please stop talking."

Millie abruptly stopped. His color slowly returned, and his breathing leveled out. "Do you want me to help you back to the office or your cabin?"

"I was heading home." Andy pushed away from the wall. "I saw you go into the stairwell and noticed someone follow behind you. It being such a late hour, something told me to make sure you were all right."

Millie's scalp tingled. "I heard someone while I was heading up the stairs. Could you tell if it was a man or a woman?"

"No. They got off on another deck. I followed them, but by the time I got there the corridor was empty. It could have been nothing." Andy motioned to the stun gun, now securely affixed to Millie's hip.

"Perhaps we're both overreacting. Let me walk you home."

"I am sorry, Andy."

"You don't need to keep apologizing."

They crossed to the other side of the ship and stopped when they reached the bridge's entrance. "Thank you for walking me home."

"You're welcome. I don't know if there's cause for alarm. To be on the safe side, I would stick to the main corridors for the rest of this voyage."

"Believe me, I will." Millie thanked him again, slipped her keycard in the slot, and eased the door open.

Late evenings on the bridge were her favorite. While daytime was a beehive of activity, at night the bridge was the complete opposite. The lights were dimmed and the only sound was the hum of the equipment.

Nic was alone on the outboard wing. She cast First Officer Craig McMasters a small smile as she slipped outside and joined her husband.

He spun around when he heard the door click shut. "Millie. You're off work early."

"Actually, I'm right on time." She bounced onto the tips of her toes and gave him a quick peck on the cheek. "I had an exciting end of the day."

"Isn't every day exciting?" Nic teased as he reached for his wife's hand.

"I accidentally tased Andy—just now, on my way home."

Nic made a choking sound. "Tased Andy?"

Millie told him how she thought she heard someone following her. "Every time I stopped, the noises stopped, so I hid behind the spa's easel board. I figured I could see who was following me. When nothing happened, I kept going."

"It was Andy?"

Millie nodded. "He said he saw someone follow me into the stairwell and was concerned." She told him whoever it was got off on another deck. "By the time Andy caught up, they were gone."

Nic's brows knitted. "That's cause for concern."

"Possibly," Millie said. "Or perhaps it was nothing but our overactive imaginations."

"I would avoid the stairwells late at night as a precaution."

"Andy and I agreed the same." Millie leaned her elbows on the railing, staring out at the starry night. "Is there any recent news on Clarissa Sinclair's death?"

"No. Patterson sent Andy's fingerprints over this morning. We haven't heard a peep."

"Far be it from me to butt in..."

Nic chuckled, and Millie shot him an annoyed look.

"Go on," Nic grinned widely.

"As I was saying, far be it from me to butt in, but why doesn't Patterson search the cabins of the people who were traveling with Sinclair?"

"Hmm." Nic made a non-committal sound.

"He already has."

"The Southampton authorities searched their belongings before they boarded the ship."

"If the strangler is one of them, he could've easily ditched any evidence, including the souvenirs he or she has been collecting," Millie pointed out.

"I don't know, Millie." Nic placed a light finger under his wife's chin and then softly kissed her. "It's getting late. We should head home. Tomorrow is a big day."

"A big day?" Millie started to ask him what he meant, but was cut off when the staff captain appeared, informing him there was a call coming in from the engineering department.

While Nic took the call, Millie headed home. She let Scout out for a quick break and then they made their way upstairs to the bedroom. She and the pup were already snuggled up in bed by the time he joined her. "Is everything all right?"

"Yes. There were some issues with the WTDs." Nic hung his jacket on the hook by the closet door and began unbuttoning his shirt.

"WTDs?"

"The watertight doors that seal in the event the ship takes on water."

"Uh-oh."

"They're working now, but the engineering supervisor wanted to give me a heads up." A low groan escaped Nic's lips as he sat on the edge of the bed. "Speaking of safety, I forgot to tell you that your exciting adventure with Sharky and the PRV was recorded. It's already been forwarded to corporate for analysis."

"Great." Millie blew air through thinned lips. "I can't wait to see how stupid I looked."

"You didn't look stupid, more like very brave. I've always wondered what it felt like to be out in the middle of the ocean and away from the ship."

"It's a completely different perspective. I never realized how hard it must be for rescuers to find someone who's gone overboard. I felt like a tiny bobber in a big ocean."

Nic squeezed his wife's hand before standing. "Thank you for being a good sport. You looked cute in the oversized rubber suit."

"I looked ridiculous. Like a big, bloated rubber ducky." Millie placed her hand behind her head and chuckled.

"Perhaps one day Donovan will show the video to you." Nic leaned in and kissed his wife's head, a mischievous twinkle in his eye. "You were barely recognizable. Besides, if it helps save a passenger's or crewmember's life, wasn't it worth it?"

He slipped inside the bathroom, and by the time he returned, Millie was already dozing off. She took her husband's hand as they said their nightly prayers, adding a prayer for the strangler's victims and for the safety of the ship's crew and passengers.

*****

Millie was off and running by the time the sun peeked over the horizon. With day three under her belt, she flew through her morning events.

During a brief break, she fixed a bowl of oatmeal, grabbed a piece of fruit and headed to a quiet corner of the ship, an area few passengers either didn't know about or didn't care to use.

She took a seat facing out, giving her an unobstructed view of the ship's massive wake. After finishing, she checked her cell phone and discovered she'd missed a call from Halbert.

Calculating the time difference since the ship and crew had shifted to East Coast time, she knew it was already the middle of the afternoon.

"Millie?"

"Hello, Halbert. How are you?"

"Good, Millie. Well...maybe not so good."

"Oh no. What's wrong? Don't tell me the strangler struck again." Although it would be horrible news, it would also mean the strangler was not on board Siren of the Seas.

"No. The police stopped by here first thing this morning." Halbert told her that one of the prints from the crime scene matched his.

"Did you point out to them you lived in the warehouse, mere steps from where Sinclair's body was found?"

"I did, but they were asking a lot of questions." Millie detected a quaver in Halbert's voice as he continued. "What if they arrest me for her murder?"

Millie pondered the question. It would be a tidy way to wrap up the case and one the authorities could use to ease the concerns of the locals, particularly if they believed the killer was on his way to Miami and the residents, at least for now, were safe.

"Where exactly did they find the fingerprint?"

"On a drink container."

"Halbert, you told me last time we talked Clarissa scratched her killer."

"Yep. That's what I heard."

"Which means they more than likely have a DNA sample of the killer's skin beneath her nails."

"Perhaps."

"Then, your DNA won't match. They have nothing concrete."

Halbert grew quiet, and she knew he was contemplating her logic. "I guess that's true." There was a muffled sound. "I'm going to write it down and tell them what you said next time they come by here."

Millie changed the subject. "How was dinner with your niece?"

"It was simply lovely, Millie. Eloise is a lot like you. She's very kind. She's going to help me get into council housing."

"That's wonderful. You might have a real roof over your head."

"I'm not so sure. Me 'n Gus are comfortable right where we are."

"But it's not safe," Millie argued. "I would feel much better knowing you were somewhere with a door and a lock." *And windows and electricity.*

"We'll see what she finds."

"And you'll think about it."

"Yes, I'll think about it."

They chatted for a few more minutes before Halbert told her he had to go. After hanging up, Millie said a small prayer for her friend's safety.

Halbert was a good man and sometimes good people needed – deserved—a break. Perhaps his niece was the break he needed.

With Halbert weighing heavily on Millie's mind, she placed her dirty dishes in the bin near the exit and took the side stairs up to the Sky Chapel.

Pastor Evans' office door was ajar, and she could see the lights were on as she gave the door a tentative knock.

The pastor, who was seated at his desk, lifted his head. "Good morning, Millie."

"Good morning, Pastor Evans." She made a move to step inside and then noticed his desk was covered with papers. "I didn't mean to bother you."

"No bother." He swept a pile off to the side. "Have a seat."

"Thanks." Millie eased into a chair.

"You look troubled."

"I am. A little. I'm sure you've heard about the Southampton Strangler and his latest victim, a news reporter who was supposed to board our ship."

"I have." The pastor solemnly nodded. "Such a sad ending to our summer abroad."

"The UK authorities believe there's a chance the killer is on board."

The pastor blinked rapidly. "On board Siren of the Seas?"

Millie nodded. "Patterson has upped security, and a note was delivered to all the passengers' cabins as well as to the ship's crew issuing a vague safety precaution."

"I got a copy of the bulletin but thought it was because we might run into some rough weather."

"That could be true too."

"There's something else," the pastor guessed.

"A passenger, a man I admire and respect, strikes me as suspicious."

"As in strangler suspicious."

"Yeah." Millie shifted uncomfortably. "He doesn't fit the serial killer profile, but there are a lot of clues pointing to him. Even suspecting him makes me feel guilty."

"Guilty but not so guilty that you aren't contemplating doing some digging around."

"Right." Millie told him about her scare the previous night and how she tased Andy, thinking he was the one who was following her in the stairwell.

The pastor pressed the tips of his fingers together. "If the killer is on board and catches wind that you're doing some digging around, you could be putting a target on your back."

"I know." Millie slowly stood. "It could already be too late."

"Does the passenger in question know your history, about your penchant for snooping?"

"He does." Millie's radio went off. "I need to get back to work."

"Be careful out there, Millie. The Southampton Strangler is clever enough to have eluded the authorities for many years."

"And he—or she—isn't about to be taken down by an assistant cruise director." Millie thanked the pastor for the chat and stepped out of the chapel. Pushing the troubling thoughts aside, she kicked into entertainer mode.

She swung by the apartment to pick up Scout after remembering he had refused to leave Millie's side that morning as she got ready for work.

She barely had enough time to unfold his stroller before he was begging to get in. She packed some snacks and water and then they headed to her first event, a round of trivia.

She recognized several attendees. Hilda was one of them. She was alone and joined another group for the competition.

The trivia ended. Millie congratulated the winners and was cleaning up when Hilda, who had stayed behind, joined them. "Hello, Scout." She patted the pup's head. "He's an adorable little dog. Why, I could just pop him into my purse and walk off with him."

"It's already happened." Millie tucked the supplies in the closet and locked the door.

Hilda's jaw dropped. "Someone took your dog?"

"They did, which is why I no longer let him out of my sight."

"How horrible."

"It was one of the scariest things I've ever gone through." Millie slid the stroller's cover all the way open and began pushing it toward the exit.

Hilda trailed behind. "I'm beginning to wonder how safe cruise ships really are. How many injuries are reported during a typical voyage?"

"I have no idea. My job is to entertain passengers." Millie forced a smile. "Now, if you'll excuse us, we have another event to host." She turned to go, and Hilda stopped her. "Wait. I have something I want to show you." She pulled her cell phone from her pocket, tapped the screen, and then handed it to Millie. "Remember how I told you someone was following me? I'm not going bonkers. Look at this."

Millie squinted her eyes as she studied the screen. It was nighttime. The ship's security lights flooded the deck and the area she recognized as the Teen Scene activity center, an area that was not currently being used since there were very few children or youths on board.

The entrance to the center was directly behind Hilda. The lights were off and the room was dark. "What am I looking at?"

"Over there, behind my right shoulder." Hilda tapped the screen to enlarge the picture. Someone was hovering nearby in the shadowy recesses. "That's my stalker."

Chapter 13

The image on Hilda's cell phone was grainy and not clear enough to make out the person's facial features. What was clear was that someone was definitely peeking around the corner, watching her. "I kept getting the feeling I was being followed, so I kept my cell phone handy. That's when I got this."

"When was this taken?"

Hilda's eyebrows furrowed as she thought about it. "It was after eleven last night. I had just gone to the buffet to grab a slice of pizza before heading to the cabin."

"And your husband..."

"Bruce. He had already gone down to the casino."

"You were alone."

"I was."

Millie did a quick calculation. The Teen Scene was in the same quadrant as the stairwell she had taken the previous evening. Was the person who was following Millie also following Hilda?

She started to put her phone away, and Millie stopped her. "Would you mind forwarding me a copy?"

"Sure. What's your cell phone number?"

Millie rattled it off. Seconds later, her phone chimed. She tapped the screen. "Got it. Thank you. Have you shown this to security?"

"You're welcome. I have. I showed it to the security guy I tracked down right after it happened. He checked the area, but there was no one around."

"I'm sorry to hear there was another incident." Millie attempted to downplay it, but her radar was engaged. Someone may have been following her...and also following Hilda Ellis.

"I'm probably not as good as you at digging into these sorts of things, but I'm becoming convinced Clarissa's killer is Thomas Windsor. As I mentioned, Clarissa was quite smitten with him. He strikes me as a bit of a gadabout, with women always following him around. Of course, not that I'm aware of his activities since he seems to make a point of avoiding me."

Millie had a sneaking suspicion Hilda had perhaps rubbed Thomas the wrong way. Not one to beat around the bush, the woman may have unintentionally insulted him.

"If you ask me, Thomas Windsor fits the strangler profile."

He didn't fit Millie's profile but, then again, she didn't know him very well, other than he was charming, polite, soft-spoken, and mysterious.

She thanked Hilda again for sending her the photo and then headed upstairs for the towel animal demonstration. Amit, who was now in charge of the event, had been practicing creating new animals in his free time.

She took her place at an adjacent table and watched as he created a purple seahorse followed by a green turtle. He finished to a round of applause.

The demonstration ended, and passengers gathered around him, asking questions and begging him to make one more.

Finally, the guests drifted off, and she helped him clean up. She had just finished when Cat radioed, asking Millie to stop by the gift shop when she had time.

Since it was down the hall, she headed there next.

Cat was near the front, helping a customer. Millie waited for her to finish before making her way over.

"That was fast."

"Amit and I were in the dining room making towel animals."

"Andy cancelled our dinner date."

"He did?"

"I think he's losing interest. The last few times I've called him, he cuts me off, telling me he'll call me back and then he never does."

"Maybe he's having a delayed reaction to me tasing him last night," Millie said.

Cat's eyes grew round as saucers. "You tased Andy?"

"It was an accident. I was on the stairwell heading home and I thought someone was following me." Millie told her she hid behind a sign. "No one showed up, so I kept going. He came up behind me and startled me. By the time I realized it was Andy, it was too late. I got him good."

"I hadn't heard that, but like I said, he's avoiding me. This whole strangler thing is bothering him. Do you think there's a chance Andy's behind the deaths?"

"No, but there's someone who is on my radar." Millie glanced around and lowered her voice. "Thomas Windsor."

"Thomas Windsor? He doesn't strike me as the killer type."

"Suspect the least suspect." Millie patted her friend's shoulder. "As far as Andy goes, it will all work out."

"I'm not so sure." Cat picked up a pen and tossed it into the holder. "I give up. I give up on men, on happiness."

"No, you don't. Andy's just in a funk."

"Well, I hope he snaps out of it."

"I've been thinking, maybe it's time to take a quick look around Windsor's cabin. I'll need to plan it so that I don't get caught."

"It will be tricky. It's not like you can wait until we're in port and sneak in there while he's gone. I can tell you where his cabin is located." With a couple clicks of the button, Cat had the information. She jotted it on a slip of paper and handed it to Millie.

"Sneaking into his cabin will be my last resort. In the meantime, keep your chin up."

It was early afternoon before Millie had another break and enough time to track down Thomas's room steward who was tidying a cabin a few doors down from his. She lightly rapped on the open door. "Hello?"

There was a muffled sound, and a woman emerged. "Hello."

"I'm sorry to bother you." Millie twirled her finger. "Are you in charge of cleaning this section of cabins?"

"I am."

"Is Thomas Windsor's cabin one of yours?"

"Yes. Mr. Windsor." The woman smiled, displaying even rows of white teeth. "He is a very nice man."

"He is." A couple came toward them, and Millie waited for them to pass by. "I was wondering if you've noticed anything unusual or odd about Mr. Windsor or his cabin."

"No." The woman reached for her clipboard. "He has always been in his cabin when I clean."

"Always in his cabin," Millie echoed.

"Some guests, they don't like the room stewards in their cabins if they aren't there."

"Does that happen often?"

She shrugged. "There are always one or two during each cruise."

"And Thomas Windsor is one of those."

"Maybe, or maybe he is not ready to leave when I am in there," she said.

"You're here twice a day...in the morning and for turndown service in the evening."

"I am."

"Mr. Windsor is in his cabin in the evenings as well?"

"Yes. But it is early, you know? He does not bother me. He lets me do my job and then I leave."

"Going back to anything odd. Have you ever noticed anything unusual about his cabin or personal belongings?"

"Odd?" The woman's brows knitted.

Millie struggled to continue her line of questioning and had another thought. "Is Mr. Windsor alone in the cabin?"

"He has a double room, but it is only him."

"So, there are no shoes, women's clothing, jewelry, or makeup on the counter or in the bathroom?"

"No. Sometimes passengers have guests in their cabin, but Mr. Windsor has not. At least, not that I have seen."

"Thank you for answering my questions." Millie turned to go. "I would appreciate it if you didn't share our conversation with anyone. It's just between the two of us."

"Yes. Just between us."

Millie thanked the woman for talking to her and then made her way upstairs. Perhaps there was a reason Thomas didn't want the room steward in his cabin when he wasn't there.

As far as she knew, the cleaning staff didn't mess with personal belongings, didn't rummage around in the closets or go through suitcases.

She thought about Patterson and his men. If the authorities had already gone through the belongings of those in Clarissa's party, there would be no reason to do it again.

As was Majestic Cruise Line's policy, luggage given to the porters was routinely checked for contraband, including smuggled alcohol, drugs, and weapons. Once the luggage was cleared and delivered to the passengers' cabins, it was rare for security to conduct a second search. It didn't make for good PR.

Millie was halfway across the ship when Cat radioed. She was on her break and asked Millie to meet her in the crew dining room. When she got there, she grabbed a glass of iced tea and joined her friend at the table. "Well?"

"I talked to Thomas's cabin steward. She hasn't noticed anything unusual. He's the only one in the cabin and always there when she's cleaning."

"So, we don't know more than we did before." Cat dipped her fry in catsup. "What makes you think there's a chance this guy might be the strangler?"

"The clues." Millie remembered a comment Thomas had made when she spoke with him right after he boarded. "He told me he was taking care of some loose ends, some family matters."

"Which doesn't strike me as odd," Cat said.

"It's also the timing. Siren of the Seas arrives in Southampton and the strangler picks up where he left off." Millie mentioned the death of Thomas's wife and a cloud of suspicion surrounding the circumstances.

"Do you think he could have been slowly poisoning his wife and then killed her but made it look like she committed suicide?"

"I don't know what to think. All I know is someone was following me last night and Hilda Ellis, a woman who was in Clarissa's group, seems to think someone is following her, as well."

The women discussed the others. Kate and Harry Moxey, Annabel and Edward Ponsford, whose family was closest to Sinclair, and then Bruce and Hilda Ellis. "Last, but not least, is Thomas Windsor. All were traveling with Clarissa."

Cat reached for her glass of lemonade. "Would it make sense to sneak into Windsor's cabin to look for clues?"

"Maybe. Going back to my biggest roadblock. I'll need to make sure he's out of his cabin." Millie snapped her fingers. "Why didn't I think of that?"

"Think of what?"

"Passengers are required to sign up for certain events." Millie tapped her scheduler watch. "All I have to do is figure out if Windsor is booked for any of those events, find someone willing to keep an eye on him and then go in for a quick search." She scrolled the screen, taking note of the events. "There are several."

"I thought I heard you mention he likes the singles' parties."

"He does. He's almost always there."

"Find out who's in charge of the next get-together, make sure he's at the event and then go in."

"It's Danielle and the next one starts at four-thirty in the Marseilles Lounge. Now all I need is someone to go in with me."

Cat wrinkled her nose. "I'm not a good snoop."

"Do you want to clear Andy's name so he can get back to his old self?"

"Yes."

"Then we need to do some digging around, starting with the suspect at the top of my list."

"All right." Cat polished off the last bite of her hotdog. "I'll go with you as long as Danielle can confirm Windsor is nowhere around."

"The good news is he's staying alone in the cabin, so we only need to keep tabs on him."

"You make it sound so easy." Cat sucked in a breath. "Promise we'll get in and get out ASAP."

"I promise." Millie gave her friend a high five. "What could possibly go wrong?"

Chapter 14

It didn't take long for Millie to track down Danielle, who was in the theater, wrapping up a line dancing class.

"Hey, Millie. What's up?"

"I need a favor. Are you hosting the happy hour Mix and Mingle Singles event today?"

Danielle rolled her eyes. "Of course. I think that's Andy's version of torture treatment for me. The more I complain, the more he schedules me for it."

"Because you do such a good job. Besides, you're cute and I'm sure the single men enjoy flirting with you."

"And I have to tell them I have a boyfriend."

"Perhaps you should invite Brody to join you when he's off duty."

"I like that idea. He can protect me from all the flirty guys." Danielle laughed. "How's your day?"

"Cat is depressed." Millie's eyes slid to the side toward Andy's office, which was directly behind the stage. "Andy's been giving her the cold shoulder. I think he's bummed the investigators are targeting him and has been avoiding her because he doesn't want to drag her into it."

"Speaking of Andy, he's looking for you." Danielle mimicked a fake British accent. "He's come up with a bloody brilliant idea."

"Great." Millie pursed her lips. "Using Andy and brilliant idea in the same sentence is never a good thing. The reason I'm asking about the singles get-together is that Cat and I were thinking about taking a quick look inside Thomas Windsor's cabin."

"And since Thomas rarely misses a singles party, you want me to keep an eye on him to make sure he's there and stays there while you take a look around."

"Bingo." Millie gave her a thumbs up. "He's at the top of my list of suspects." She mentioned the stairwell incident. "At first, I thought Hilda Ellis was imagining it when she said someone was following her. Now, I'm not so sure."

"Why would someone be following you?" Danielle asked.

Millie shrugged. "Because if the strangler is on board, he or she might suspect that I'm poking my nose into the deaths and is trying to scare me."

"Or even worse, trying to take you out. I would be careful."

"After last night, I will. So, will you help Cat and me?"

"Of course. I wish I was the one going with you instead of playing lookout." Danielle shifted her weight. "I'll need to tag team with my co-host. These events get chaotic and it's going to be nearly impossible for me to watch Windsor the entire time."

"Who's your co-host?"

"Let me check." Danielle whipped her cell phone out of her pocket and scrolled through the screen. "It's Felix."

"Perfect." Millie clapped her hands. "That ought to be fun."

"Felix can liven up any event. I'll ask him to help."

"You're the best. I knew I could count on you." Millie turned to go, and Danielle stopped her. "Wait. Don't forget about Andy. He's in his office. At least he was last time I checked."

Millie thanked her and then headed to the back of the stage. A large beam of bright light emanated from Andy's half-open door. She gave the door a light rap and stuck her head around the corner. "Hey, Andy. Danielle said you were looking for me."

"I am. Come in." Andy reached behind him and grabbed a box she recognized as the passengers' comments and suggestions box. "I've come up with a new and exciting event and it involves you."

"New and exciting?"

"It also involves Annette. Let me see if she's free so I can tell you both at the same time." Andy grabbed his cell phone and tapped the screen.

"Hello?"

"Annette. Andy here. I have you on speaker."

"Okay."

"I was wondering if you had a minute to meet with Millie and me in my office."

"Why?"

"I'll explain when you get here."

There was a moment of hesitation before Annette promised she was on her way.

"Splendid. We'll see you soon."

Millie watched as Andy sifted through the stack of cards. "I thought you moved to online comment cards. Trying to save paper and all."

"I have. I get online suggestions and feedback, but we still get our fair share of these. In fact, I forgot all about emptying the bin until a couple hours ago."

"You came up with your brilliant plan in a couple hours?"

"It's been in the back of my mind for a while. Reading some of the recent suggestions confirmed it."

Millie stared at the stack. "You have quite a few."

"The bin was almost full. I've been tracking the suggestions for new events, and the one I'm about to pitch to you and Annette is one that keeps popping up."

Footsteps echoed outside the office.

Annette appeared in the doorway and Andy waved her in. "Thank you for getting down here so fast."

"You caught me at the right time." Annette took a seat next to Millie. "What's up?"

"I was telling Millie, I've gone through all the passenger comments and suggestions, and one particular event keeps getting mentioned." Andy paused, letting the anticipation build.

"And..." Annette twirled her hand.

"I want to offer a cooking class."

"A cooking class," Millie echoed.

"Yes. It's brilliant, really. Annette can host the class with the help of an assistant or two. Perhaps you and Amit. It will feature items only available at our specialty restaurants. If the attendees enjoy the dishes, my thought is it will entice them to book the specialty dining restaurants. Sales have been lagging lately."

"Because the British Isles were port-intensive. Most people weren't even back on board for a proper dinner," Millie pointed out.

"Exactly. So, I figured now that the passengers are stuck on board the ship, we could test the cooking class, perhaps pimp the specialty dining to boost sales and revenue."

Millie's eyes narrowed. "What's in it for you—or more precisely—for the entertainment department?" Andy was a for-profit boss. He loved to keep his department's coffers full of cash. There had to be a catch.

"I was thinking we could offer a discount coupon for the dining." Andy pointed to Millie. "That's where you come in. While Annette is feeding them delicious gourmet dishes, you can upsell them on the restaurants."

"All the while lining your pockets." Millie shook her head.

Andy patted the pile of comment cards. "We need to give passengers what they want, and they want a cooking class."

"Well?" Annette turned to Millie. "I'm not typically keen on Andy's ideas, but this one appears to have potential."

"What do you mean you're not keen on my ideas?"

Annette ignored his question. "We could host it in one of the specialty dining restaurants to create a unique ambience. I think Andy might be onto something here."

"It does have potential." Millie motioned to Andy. "Would you charge a per-person fee and limit the size of the class by making them register in advance?"

"That's why you're here. I need your input. If we make it exclusive, either by charging a small per-person fee or by signing up and limiting the number of attendees, we'll create a perceived scarcity, and Voila!" Andy snapped his fingers. "Instant success."

"I think limiting the class, at least during the trial period, makes the most sense," Annette said.

"Ditto. If this turns out to be as popular as you think it will be, we want the attendees to have a positive experience, where they can see the dishes being made, interact with the ship's chef on a more personal level, making it a more intimate event," Millie said.

"I like it." Andy grabbed his yellow pad and began scribbling. There was some discussion on a name for the event, the venue, and cap for the number of attendees. "How about Appetizers with Annette?"

"Or Siren of the Seas' Savory Dishes," Millie said.

"I think Andy Wants to Make a Quick Buck sounds catchy," Annette joked.

"Creative Chef sounds fun."

"Or Culinary Creations by Annette," Andy suggested.

"I like it. Culinary Creations by Annette," Millie said. "Write me into the schedule, and I'll leave the details up to you and Annette."

"I can squeeze our first event in tomorrow, if that works."

"Perfect." Andy jotted a few more notes. "Culinary Creations by Annette, tomorrow in The Vine restaurant at two o'clock."

"I'll come up with elegant yet easy dishes."

"Dishes we could serve in the specialty dining," Andy reminded her.

"Right." Annette gave a thumbs up. "Limit the list to twenty or less. The restaurant can easily accommodate that number with a head table near the front for the cooking presentation."

"I'll announce the sign-ups to be done at the excursions desk by the end of today and will have coupons printed for Millie to pass out." Andy clicked the end of his pen. "What do you think about inviting our sommelier, Pierre LeBlanc, to the event?"

"To sell expensive bottles of wine while they're partaking of gourmet goodies?" Millie grinned. "Andy, Andy, Andy."

"Never miss an opportunity, that's my motto."

Annette left first, promising to give Andy the names of the dishes she planned to prepare before the end of the day, and headed out.

Millie's app alerted her to her next event. "I need to get going." She tapped the screen and scrolled to the bottom. "Part of my evening schedule is gone."

"I gave you a few hours off."

"Why?"

Andy averted his gaze.

Millie said the first thing that popped into her head. "Am I in trouble?"

"No, unless there's something you need to confess."

Millie thought about her upcoming snooping plan. "Not yet."

"I can't say." Andy quickly changed the subject. "By the way, I found an envelope in the comment box with your name on it." He rummaged around inside before handing her a small envelope.

"Thanks." Millie glanced at the front before tucking it into her pocket. It wasn't unusual for passengers to leave thank-you notes for crewmembers or the ship's staff, particularly if the person went above and beyond their duties and the passenger wanted to express their appreciation. "For the record, I think the culinary class is a great idea."

"I'm excited to see how it does."

After exiting the office, Millie called Cat to finalize their game plan and then made her rounds, counting the minutes until the mix and mingles event was scheduled to begin. With twenty minutes and counting, she did a deck check of Thomas's cabin area.

Since cabin tidying was mid-morning and turndown was during the dinner hours, timing would be crucial in ensuring she and Cat got in and out without running into the room steward.

With a quick run through, she headed upstairs. Cat, along with one of the other store employees, was inside. She waited off to the side for her friend to join her.

"Are you ready for this?"

"No." Cat clutched her stomach. "I feel like throwing up. What if we get caught?"

"We always run that risk. Danielle is going to confirm Windsor is at the single's party before we go in."

"Good. Good. What about the room stewards?"

"We'll miss them if we get in and out." Millie reached for her cell phone, making sure she hadn't missed a text or call. She noticed the note Andy had given her, the one he'd found in the comment box, and pulled it out.

"What's that?"

"Someone left a note for me in the passengers' comments box." On closer inspection, she noticed her name was carefully printed in block letters, "Millie Armati."

Millie turned the envelope over and ran her finger under the edge before lifting the flap. She began to feel lightheaded as she flipped it open and read the two words printed in the same bold block letters.

Chapter 15

Danielle picked up the pace and began jogging to the lounge where the Mix and Mingle Singles event was being held. Felix was standing by the door, chatting with one of the servers, when she arrived.

"Danielle," Felix gushed. "When I found out we were co-hosting the M&M, I said to myself, 'Felix, you have got to ask Danielle who creates that amazing platinum blond hair of hers.' Do you go to one of those adorable stylists in the salon?"

"No. Never colored it in my life." Danielle ran her fingers through her hair. "God gave me these luscious locks," she joked. "You can't seriously be considering lightening your hair. Your color suits you to a 't.'"

"I need a new look." Felix snapped his fingers, swiveling his hips as he twirled in a slow circle.

"We're heading back to the States, and my homies in Miami are waiting for our return. I thought I would show the South Beach Scene what a cultured, sophisticated world traveler I've become. The old me is so...dull and boring."

Danielle chuckled. "Felix, you have never been dull a day in your life, and you don't have a boring bone in your body. Besides, the hair doesn't make the man. It's your natural sparkle."

"You're too sweet." Felix grasped Danielle's shoulders and air-kissed her. "Thank you for the pep talk, lovey."

"If you decide to go for a new 'do,' I would consult with the stylist first. Your hair is such a dark, natural shade, you don't want it to turn orange."

"Orange?" Felix pressed a hand to his chest, his eyes widening in horror. "Do you think that would happen?"

"I don't know, but it's worth finding out first."
Danielle glanced at the crowd that was starting to
gather. "It's time to get this party started."

"You handle the mix and I'll handle the mingle."
Felix turned to go, and Danielle stopped him.
"Millie asked for our help. We need to keep an eye
on Thomas Windsor. Do you know who he is?"

"No."

Danielle craned her neck, catching a glimpse of
Windsor, who had just arrived. "He's over
there...the mature gentleman with the silver locks.
Do you see him?"

Felix followed her gaze. "I think so. He's to the
right of the entrance."

"Correct. We need to make sure he doesn't leave
the event early."

"Why?" Felix held up a hand. "Never mind. If
this involves Millie, I'm certain I don't want the
details."

"The less you know, the better."

"I shall follow him around like a lost puppy."

"Good, and I'll try to keep track of him too." Danielle darted to the door and unlocked it as she began greeting the guests. The lounge filled at a rapid rate, reaching capacity before it even started.

While Danielle stood by the door greeting the guests, Felix mingled. He flitted from group to group, starting a conversation to break the ice before moving on to the next.

A trio of musicians arrived and set up near the back of the small stage. Danielle, noting most attendees were a more mature crowd, briefly consulted with the musicians and they began playing a mixture of sixties and seventies music.

The dance floor filled, and Danielle stopped by the bar to check on the drinks and snacks. With the party in full swing, and confirming Thomas Windsor was in attendance, she made her way to the quietest corner she could find.

She unclipped her radio and turned her back to the crowd. "Millie, do you copy?"

"Go ahead, Danielle."

"The mix and mingle party is in full swing. You should stop by if you have time."

"Okay. I'll try," Millie promised. "Do you have a full house?"

"Yes. There are a lot of familiar faces. In fact, Thomas Windsor is here. He asked if you were co-hosting with me."

"I see. Thanks for the invite. I'll see what I can do."

"Great. If I were you, I would do it sooner, rather than later."

"Gotcha. I have something else to take care of, but it shouldn't take long. In fact, I'm there now so I had better get going."

"Over and out." Danielle replaced her radio. She had given Millie the all-clear to sneak into

Windsor's cabin, who was now trapped near the bar, surrounded by several women. "Hurry, Millie. Something about this gives me a bad vibe," she whispered under her breath.

Danielle crossed the room and began making small talk, chatting about the voyage and their port stop in Bermuda.

"Argh!" An anguished cry echoed from across the room. It was coming from the direction of the dance floor. Danielle excused herself, weaving through the crowd as she hurried to the stage.

Several onlookers formed a semi-circle around a woman who was sprawled out on the floor, her leg twisted at an odd angle.

Felix caught up with Danielle and he knelt next to the woman. While he ascertained the extent of the guest's injuries, Danielle radioed for medical.

Thankfully, two of the emergency staff members arrived promptly.

Danielle nudged the crowd back, making room for the medical team, who wheeled a wheelchair into the lounge. After helping the woman into the chair, Danielle escorted them to the door.

"We'll take her down to medical for an examination."

The woman clutched her chest. "I'm having chest pains."

"Get going." Danielle held the door and watched as they hustled out of the lounge to the nearby bank of elevators.

The party resumed, but at a more subdued level. Danielle's eyes slowly scanned the lounge, searching for Thomas Windsor. He was nowhere in sight.

She took a tentative step, her eyes scanning again.

"Danielle." Felix hurried over. "I can't find Thomas Windsor."

"Me either." Danielle made her way over to the group she'd last seen him with. "Is Thomas still here?"

One of them shook her head. "No. He left right after that woman got injured on the dance floor."

Chapter 16

"What is it?" Cat asked. "Your face is as white as a ghost."

Millie handed her friend the note.

"You're next. What does this mean?"

Instead of answering, Millie reached for her radio and then stopped. "Andy told me he cleared out the customer comment bin and found this note in there."

"How long has it been since he emptied the bin?"

"I don't know."

"Maybe you should find out."

Millie stared at her friend, her mind refusing to register what *might* have happened. Andy was from the UK. Andy was in the vicinity at the time the strangler struck. He was in the stairwell the previous night when Millie suspected she was being followed.

Her eyes fell to the diamond and charm bracelet Cat was wearing, the one Andy had given her. She needed to find out what the uni student's charm bracelet looked like. "We need to find out if the ship was in port at the time of the murders."

"Millie." Cat clutched her arm. "Andy took a leave. Remember? He left the ship while his sister, Sarah, was on board. The Southampton port area is where most of the strangler's victims were found."

"And Halbert swears he caught a glimpse of the strangler. I always wondered if perhaps the serial killer hadn't, at some point in time, worked on the docks or on a ship, maybe even a cargo ship."

"Or a cruise ship." Cat studied the note. "What if Andy wrote this note? What if he found out you were snooping around in the strangler case and is concerned you're getting too close to the truth?"

"Millie, do you copy?" It was Danielle. She gave her the green light, letting her know that Thomas Windsor was at the party.

Millie signed off and then clipped her radio to her belt. "We'll have to put that on the back burner. For now, we need to get inside Windsor's cabin while the getting is good."

Since they were mere steps away from his door, it was a brisk stroll to his cabin, port side and aft of the ship.

With a quick glance to make sure the coast was clear, Millie slid her master keycard into the slot. She waited for the *ding* and then eased the door open.

The interior was cool and quiet. The cabin's curtains were drawn, and only a sliver of light escaped through a gap in the center.

Cat quietly closed the door behind them. "It's dark in here."

"We're in. We might as well turn the lights on." Millie flipped the switch, giving her eyes a moment to adjust to the brightness. The room was tidy, as in neat as a pin. A pair of polished black dress shoes were tucked under the counter.

A gray suit hung from the closet door. A musky aroma, mingled with an earthy scent, lingered in the air.

"I like his cologne," Cat whispered. "It smells nice."

"It does. It's probably some natural allure called, 'Animal Magnetism,'" Millie joked. "Let's split up. I'll take the bathroom."

"What are we looking for?"

"Souvenirs the strangler collected. A blue tennis shoe, a pair of prescription glasses and..." Millie paused, bracing herself for Cat's reaction at one of the items she'd heard the strangler had taken. "A charm bracelet."

"You're kidding." Cat touched her bracelet. "Andy's the strangler."

"No. I mean, we don't know that. I don't know what the bracelet looks like. I have a hunch the strangler took a pair of prescription glasses and a woman's blue tennis shoe." Millie nudged Cat toward the center of the cabin. "We'll deal with the rest after we're out of here."

She stepped inside the compact bathroom. Similar to the main cabin, it was tidy. Even the used washcloth was neatly hung on the towel bar. The contents of the medicine cabinet were arranged largest to smallest, left to right with the labels all facing out.

There was no sign of the items in question. Millie exited the bathroom and found Cat poking around inside the nightstand. She opened the closet door and wasn't surprised to discover Thomas's clothes were organized by item and color. His shoes lined the floor...dress shoes first, followed by sandals and then slippers.

She checked the pockets of his pants and shirts and then consulted her watch. They had been inside the cabin for almost ten minutes, reaching what she considered the maximum amount of acceptable snoop time.

"Cat," she whispered.

"Huh?"

"We gotta go." Millie motioned for her to join her near the door. "I didn't find anything."

"Me either." Cat turned her thumb down. "If he's hiding the stuff, he's doing an excellent job."

"We'll have to move on to Plan B."

"Which is?"

"I don't know yet." Millie heard the sound of muffled voices in the hall and pressed a finger to her lips. It was a male voice. A female voice replied. The doorknob rattled.

Cat dove under the bed. Millie hit the floor and rolled in behind her only seconds before the cabin door opened.

Millie clamped a hand over her mouth, watching as a pair of steel-toed work boots appeared.

"I am certain, Mr. Patterson." Millie recognized the voice as Thomas's room steward. "I have been keeping a close eye on Mr. Windsor's cabin. He left a short time ago. Not long after, I noticed two people going into this cabin."

"You didn't see them leave?"

"No, sir. I've been standing guard watching ever since I radioed you that I saw someone."

Millie cringed when she heard the bathroom door open and shut, followed by the closet doors. "And it wasn't Mr. Windsor?"

"I'm almost certain at least one of them was a crewmember. The woman was wearing a navy-blue suit."

"Navy-blue suit." Patterson's shoes shifted. Millie gritted her teeth at the sight of a pair of knees and then, finally, Patterson's face.

Their eyes locked.

"Millie Armati." His eyes slowly shifted to Cat, who was now breathing heavily, nearly hyperventilating. "Catherine Wellington. I would ask you what you're doing, but I think I have a pretty good idea." He briefly closed his eyes and motioned for them to exit their hiding spot.

Millie crawled out from under the bed first.

Cat, who was still breathing heavily, joined them. "I'm. We're sorry. We figured it wouldn't hurt to take a quick look around Mr. Windsor's cabin while he was away."

Patterson arched a brow. "And *how,* pray tell, did you know Windsor was out of his cabin?"

"He's...he's attending the Mix and Mingles Singles party in the lounge," Cat stuttered. "We didn't touch anything."

"Really?" Patterson wagged his finger at her. "You touched the door handle, the closet door, the bathroom door. I'm sure you touched the drawer handles."

"It was a quick look around," Millie argued. "In and out. No harm, no foul."

"Entering a passenger's cabin is against company policy. The only ones who should be in this cabin are the passenger and the room steward. I'm writing both of you up." Patterson led the way out of the cabin and into the hall. "Follow me."

Millie hung back, casting Cat an apologetic look as they followed Patterson and the woman into the corridor. The room steward headed in the opposite direction as Millie and Cat trudged along behind the head of security.

They reached the bank of elevators and waited until the doors opened. Thomas Windsor stepped out, nearly colliding with the trio.

"Excuse me. Hello, Millie. Cat." Windsor shot Patterson an inquisitive look, and Millie guessed it was because of Patterson's uniform and the fact he wasn't smiling.

"Good afternoon, Thomas." Millie swallowed hard, wondering for a fleeting second if Patterson would rat them out, and then quickly dismissed it. Their punishment would be swift and severe but would not involve a passenger.

Patterson waited until Thomas disappeared around the corner. "I think an elevator ride is the fitting beginning of the punishment I plan to mete out for your impulsive and rash actions."

"Of course." Millie was the last to enter the elevator, watching as he jabbed the down button.

"I'm sure I don't have to point out to you that had I not busted you, Mr. Windsor would have reached his cabin by now and you would have been caught by him."

"We were on our way out when you showed up," Millie muttered under her breath.

Patterson shot her daggers, and Millie shrank back, wondering what the reprimand would entail...being put on probation, turning in her all-access keycard, restricting her online database access. The list was long and none of it struck Millie as appealing.

The elevator doors opened, and they exited into the crew-only area when Millie's radio went off. It was Danielle, sounding a little frantic. "Millie, do you copy?"

"Danielle?" Patterson guessed.

"Yes."

"Your other accomplice?"

Millie gave a small nod of her head.

"May I?" Patterson didn't wait for an answer as he reached for her radio. "Go ahead, Danielle."

There was a brief pause. "Is Millie around?"

"She's standing next to me, on her way to my office for breaking company policy. Both her and Cat."

"Crud."

"Crud is right. What do you want?"

"To let her know the Silver Fox has left the den, but I guess it doesn't matter now."

"We ran into the Silver Fox near the elevators."

"Ohhhh....kay. I'll be going now." Danielle abruptly signed off.

Cat and Millie had to hustle to keep up with Patterson, who was moving at breakneck speed down the long corridor.

They reached the head of the security department's office and he waited for them to step inside before closing the door behind them. He motioned for them to have a seat.

Millie perched on the edge while Cat took the one closest to the exit. Her expression teetered between sheer panic and looking as if she was going to bolt.

"I suppose it's time to get Andy and Donovan down here since this matter involves their employees." Instead of radioing them, he called them on their cell phones.

Millie cringed as he told Andy it was rather important that he join him in his office as soon as possible. After having a similar conversation with Donovan, he leaned back in his chair, pressing the tips of his fingers together, and Millie could only imagine the level of punishment he was contemplating.

"I'm sorry, Patterson," Cat said.

"Apology accepted, although it doesn't mean I won't issue you a warning for your behavior."

Cat's shoulders slumped. "A warning?"

"Yes. I'll remove the warning from your file after thirty days, assuming you don't commit a second disciplinary offense."

239

"I won't."

"I think a warning sounds fair," Millie said.

Patterson leaned forward, placing his elbows on his knees. "Cat's punishment is a warning, which I feel is appropriate considering I believe you were the instigator of the incident."

"I was."

"Which means your punishment needs to be something you'll remember. Something painful that will make you think twice before completely disregarding company policy again."

There was a knock on the door. Andy, closely followed by Donovan, appeared. "You're just in time."

While Patterson rifled through his filing cabinet, he briefly filled the men in on what had transpired. "I'm sure it won't be hard for either of you to surmise whose idea it was."

Millie lowered her head as Andy's eyes bore into her.

"I'm disappointed in you, Cat," Donovan said.

"I'm sorry, Donovan," Cat whispered. "It seemed like a good idea at the time."

Patterson cleared his throat as he removed a file folder with Cat's name on it. "The fact I have a folder on you should be enough for you to think twice about pulling another stunt like that." He filled out a form and then handed it to Donovan. "If this is acceptable and we're in agreement, you can give it to Cat to sign."

Donovan perused the sheet and passed it to Cat.

She scanned the sheet, signed her name at the bottom and then handed it to Patterson.

"You're free to go." He placed it inside her folder.

"What about Millie?"

"She's next." Patterson pulled two sheets of paper from his desk and began writing. It seemed to take forever, and Millie could feel her armpits grow damp.

Finally, he stopped writing. He took his time studying each sheet before handing both to Andy. "Feel free to add anything else you can think of."

Andy made a clicking sound with his teeth and then shook his head. "I believe this is sufficient reprimand," he said before handing the papers to Millie.

Millie slipped her reading glasses on and studied the first. Instead of a warning, hers was a sixty-day probation. She signed the sheet and then reached for the second. "You've got to be kidding me."

Chapter 17

"This isn't fair." Millie waved the sheet of paper in the air. "I'll take my sixty-day probation, but I don't have the mental fortitude to work in guest services."

"I think it's an appropriate punishment," Andy said. "I'll find someone else to host trivia while you spend a few afternoons handling customer complaints. Assuming Donovan approves of you working behind the desk, dealing with irate passengers."

Donovan shrugged. "Fine with me. It will give Millie a sampling of one of the most challenging jobs on board the ship. I'll have her work alongside Nikki Tan."

"For how long?"

Patterson and Andy exchanged a quick glance. "I think a couple days is sufficient punishment. That, along with the sixty-day probation."

Millie reluctantly signed the paper, grumbling under her breath as she handed it to Patterson. "I'm being targeted by some crazed serial killer and you're punishing me by making me work one of the worst jobs on the ship."

"What do you mean you're being targeted by a crazed serial killer?" Patterson asked.

Millie removed the small envelope from her pocket and handed it to him.

He pulled out the single sheet of paper, his expression growing grim as he studied the "you're next," note. "Where did you get this?"

"Andy gave it to me. He said it came from the suggestion box."

Patterson's eyes shot up. "When?"

"This morning. I hadn't cleaned it out since we left Southampton," Andy said. "I had no idea what it was. Sometimes the passengers leave nice notes for staff in the comment box. I thought it was a thank-you note."

Patterson passed it to Donovan. "This throws a whole new light on things."

"Does this mean you'll forget about the formal reprimand?" Millie asked.

"Absolutely not. The note still doesn't excuse your behavior. We can't have you sneaking into passengers' cabins on a whim."

"It wasn't a whim," Millie argued. "We had a plan in place." She started to say something else, but the look on Patterson's face stopped her. "Fine. Guest services it is."

There was some discussion regarding increasing patrols, including in the crew areas, before Patterson dismissed the women.

Cat waited until they were out of the office and at the end of the hall. "That went well."

"Maybe for you. A temporary warning is a slap on the wrist."

"True. You staying out of trouble for two months will be nearly impossible," Cat joked.

"Especially now with everything that's going on." Millie slowed. "I've focused my attention on Andy and Thomas Windsor, but there are other people Clarissa was traveling with that I need to take a closer look at."

"The ship's database would be the most logical place to start."

"I was thinking the same thing." Millie accompanied Cat to the gift shop before starting her next event. She ran into Danielle, briefly filling her in on what had happened.

"I figured you got busted when Patterson answered your radio call."

"He was ticked when he found us hiding under Thomas's bed. Part of my punishment is working at the guest services desk for a couple days."

Danielle wrinkled her nose. "Bummer."

"Bummer is right. Looking back, I should've known better." Millie patted her pocket and the "you're next" note. What did it mean? Was it a veiled threat? Was it linked to whoever followed her into the stairwell?

Was it a coincidence that Andy was in the vicinity when the stairwell incident occurred? He was also the one who gave her the "you're next" note. She shared her concerns with Danielle, stopping short of accusing Andy of being responsible. "I don't know what to think."

"It seems a lot of what's happened to you points to Andy."

Millie fleetingly wondered how long it would take for word of the incident and Patterson's disciplinary actions to get back to her husband.

"Have you assembled a list of potential suspects?"

"I jotted down some notes. I can check the manifest and ship's information on each passenger, but I need more." Millie snapped her fingers. "I know the perfect person who can help. Isla."

"How can Isla help?"

"Since she manages shore excursions and onboard bookings, she has access to passengers' payments and reservations." It took a few minutes for Millie and Danielle to track Isla down. They found her on the sports deck chatting with the ship's golf pro.

"Hello, ladies. I haven't seen either of you around much since we left Southampton."

"We've been busy." Millie got right to the point. "The UK authorities believe the Southampton Strangler may be on board the ship. Someone has been following me and possibly a passenger since we left port." Millie handed Isla the note. "This note was in the comment box."

Isla read the note and let out a low whistle. "Whoa. And you think it may be the strangler trying to scare you?"

"Or worse. Cat and I searched the cabin of the number one suspect on board and got caught by Patterson. Red-handed, as in—in the passenger's cabin and hiding under his bed."

Isla's eyes grew round as saucers. "I bet he wasn't happy."

"I'm on a sixty-day probation and working desk duty at guest services for the next couple days."

"That job can be brutal." If anyone would know, it would be Isla since the excursions desk was directly across from guest services. "At least once a day someone is throwing a hissy fit about something."

"Great. I can't wait," Millie groaned. "There's one more piece of the puzzle linking the latest victim to this ship. She was booked on this voyage."

"I heard they found the woman's body in the park across from the port. It's downright scary how close these murders have happened."

"Which leads me to the reason why I'm here. I'm hoping to find out a little more about the woman's traveling companions, their habits, what they're doing while on board."

"I can help you with that since the onboard reservations flow through the excursions department."

"Would it be possible to take a quick look at them?"

"Of course." Isla led them down the side steps, not stopping until they reached the excursion's desk. The trio squeezed past a staff member who was assisting a passenger, making their way to the other end.

Isla swiped her keycard through the computer's side slot and entered her access code. "Who do you want to start with?"

"Edward and Annabel Ponsford," Millie said. "P-o-n-s-f-o-r-d."

"Got it." Isla tapped the keys and pressed enter. She rattled off their cabin number. "Their folio is linked to several others."

"The other parties of interest," Millie said.

"That will make things easy." Isla clicked on a button, pulling up the Ponsford's profiles.

Millie slipped her reading glasses on and studied their information. It listed their address, dates of birth, and an emergency contact. At the bottom of the screen was a "reservation" button. "What's this?"

"A record of the Ponsford's onboard bookings, both previous and upcoming." Isla clicked the button. A long list of events appeared. Nothing looked unusual or noteworthy. After finishing, Isla exited the screen.

"Bruce and Hilda Ellis are next."

The trio grew quiet as they scanned the couple's information. Millie noticed they lived in the same town as the Ponsfords. Unlike the Ponsfords, the Ellis's activity and reservation screens were empty. As in...completely empty.

"It looks as if they haven't booked anything," Isla said, "which isn't necessarily noteworthy. Some passengers don't."

"According to Hilda, her husband hangs out in the casino." Millie tapped her chin. "Reading between the lines of what Hilda has told me, they don't spend a lot of time together."

"What's going on back here?"

Millie shifted her gaze. Donovan stood on the opposite side of the desk, staring down at them. "Danielle and I are chatting with Isla while she's on break."

"Chatting with Isla or snooping?"

Danielle feigned indignation. "Are you always suspicious of motives?"

"When it involves Millie, the answer is yes." Donovan pinned Isla with a stare. "Isla?"

Isla shrank back. "I was just, uh, showing Danielle and Millie how the reservation system works. They've never seen it before."

Donovan leaned in. "Turn the monitor so I can see."

Isla shot Millie a nervous glance as she slowly shifted the monitor.

"That's what I thought." Donovan briefly closed his eyes. "Let me guess. This couple is part of the group being investigated."

"They are," Millie said. "Looking at passengers' records isn't against company policy."

"True, but you're already treading on thin ice."

"Duly noted." Millie met Donovan's gaze. "Is there anything else?"

"No." He gave her a warning shake of his head before stalking off.

Millie watched him step behind the guest services desk and disappear inside his office.

"You're on the radar now," Danielle said.

"Always." Millie sighed heavily. "At least we're almost done."

Last, but not least, were Kate and Harry Moxey. "They're in a suite and only a few doors down from the Ponsford's balcony cabin," Danielle noted.

"Good catch." Millie studied the screen and then waited for Isla to click on their "reservation" button. "They've spent some bucks in Celebrations, the ship's store for hosting private events. Too bad we can't see what they purchased."

"Says who?" Isla double-clicked on the Celebrations link. A list of liquor, appetizers, and snacks popped up. A date was next to each of the items.

"Whoa Nellie," Danielle blurted out. "These two are partiers. What is all of this stuff?"

"Goodies ordered from Celebrations and delivered to the Moxey's suite." Isla's finger trailed down the list. "It looks as if it's party time at the Moxey's every evening."

"I'm not surprised," Millie said. "They're very social and attend a lot of the mix and mingle events."

Danielle snapped her fingers. "I know who they are. They're at every single single's event. It strikes me as a little odd that a married couple would attend a singles event."

"It does me too, but to each his own. I wonder who attends their little get-togethers." Millie drummed her fingers on the desk.

"Wonder no more." Isla grinned as she tapped the button at the bottom of the screen.

"Celebrations offers passengers a nifty little tool. If you're throwing a party, all you have to do is let them know who you want to invite, the time and location of your get-together and they'll send out electronic invitations."

"That's cool," Danielle said. "So, you go to Celebrations, order your party goodies, give them the list of names and they send out invitations."

"Electronically, delivered right through the ship's app directly to their cell phone."

"What technology can't do these days." Millie shook her head in amazement.

Isla tapped the screen. "It looks as if the Moxeys are having another party. It starts in a couple hours."

"Who did they invite?" Millie leaned in as she studied the list of names. The one at the very top caught her eye. Captain Niccolo Armati. "The Moxeys invited Nic. I think I found my way inside their suite without getting into trouble."

Chapter 18

Millie thanked Isla for the information before steering Danielle away from the desk and to a quiet corner. "I need to figure out a way to talk Nic into making an appearance at the Moxey's party."

"Good luck." Danielle chuckled as she patted Millie's shoulder. "I need to get back to work."

"Thanks. I'll need it." Millie practiced a few versions of how she would pitch the party to her husband, who made a point not to attend private passenger functions. Mainly because it was a timing issue, not to mention he was frequently invited to private events.

She ran a couple scenarios through her head and then decided to bite the bullet.

Nic answered her call, and she could tell he'd already heard about her reprimand. "Hello, dear."

"Hello, Nic. I thought I would check in to see how your day is going."

"Fine. I met with Patterson and Andy earlier and was entertained by your latest exploit."

"I wouldn't call it an exploit. Exploration might be a more fitting description."

"Exploit. Exploration." Nic let out a heavy sigh. "What was the purpose of putting yourself in such a predicament? Surely, you're aware Patterson and the security department have eyes and ears on the ground, keeping tabs on Sinclair's traveling companions."

"Yes. I'm sure he is—they are—but sometimes things are overlooked. Besides, if Thomas Windsor knew he and his belongings were being searched, he would do his best to hide potential evidence."

"You figured you could catch him off guard and had a better chance of uncovering something they weren't able to find."

"Pretty much," Millie admitted.

258

"I also heard about the note and would like to see it when you have time to stop by."

"My dinner break is starting soon."

"Dinner together sounds nice," Nic said. "In fact, I convinced Andy to give you a few hours off, since you've been putting in some long days. I thought we could both use a little downtime."

Millie's heart skipped a beat. The timing was perfect. Now, all she had to do was convince her husband to spend a few minutes at the Moxey's party. She promised she would meet him on the bridge within the hour and ended the call.

She rehearsed several pitches about why they should attend the cocktail party, but none of them came across as anything less than a veiled attempt to snoop.

Nic was a "cut and dried" kind of guy, and she decided a direct approach was best. Perhaps pointing out the note was a veiled threat and getting to the bottom of who might be behind it was a priority.

Since Millie had texted ahead, Nic was already home and waiting for her. "Dinner together is a rare treat. I've decided to save the speech and not ruin what little time we have alone together by lecturing you."

"Thank you." Millie clasped a hand to her chest. "Besides, I think my probation and being assigned to guest services is punishment enough."

"So, if we dine in, what sounds good?" Nic pulled his wife into his arms. "An Italian meal from The Vine sounds tempting, or perhaps the Bamboo Wok. We haven't had Chinese food in a while."

"Both sound delicious. I found out you've been invited to Kate and Harry Moxey's cabin for cocktail hour, which starts in a few minutes. I was wondering if you would like to pop in to show them what a personable captain you are."

"Kate and Harry Moxey. Weren't they Clarissa Sinclair's traveling companions?"

"They were."

"Why would you want to attend their cocktail party? As a rule, we never attend private functions."

"I'm almost certain someone in their party is responsible for Sinclair's death, that the strangler is on board the ship and I'm being targeted." Millie removed the note from her pocket and handed it to her husband. "This is the note Andy found in the comment box."

Nic studied it, a somber expression on his face. "Why would the strangler target you?"

"I don't know. What I do know is Hilda Ellis has a shadowy picture of the person who was following her. She's part of the Sinclair group. What's happening to her is now happening to me."

Nic started to pace. "How can attending a cocktail party help?"

"I don't know. Perhaps something is said, some clue slips out. I'm betting all persons of interest will attend the party. What better way to find out?" Millie had racked her brain, wondering why she was being targeted, too. "Maybe the connection is Halbert Pennyman. We're friends. Halbert swears he's seen the strangler. Maybe the strangler thinks I'm onto him and he's targeting me."

"It's a stretch." Nic abruptly stopped. "As far as we know, the authorities still haven't linked the victims. There's no thread of commonality, no rhyme or reason on how the killer picks his victims."

"Not true." Millie lifted a finger. "Clarissa Sinclair was a reporter. Only hours before her death she called her office, claiming to have information on the strangler. I think she was a victim, but perhaps not an intended one." She laid out her theory, how she believed Sinclair knew her killer. "Once the strangler discovered he was about to be exposed, he had to act fast, to get rid of Sinclair."

"In his haste, he may have made a mistake."

"Right. And now, if the strangler is on board the ship, he or she is targeting Hilda Ellis and possibly even me."

Nic silently eyed his wife. "All right. I'll go to the cocktail party, but I don't plan on staying long. I would rather spend what little time I have off alone with my naughty wife."

Millie threw her arms around Nic's neck. "Thank you for agreeing to go. We'll stay for an hour, tops, and then come back here to enjoy a romantic dinner for two."

*****

By the time Nic and Millie arrived, the party was in full swing. The door to the suite was wide open, and they made their way inside. A server hurriedly approached and offered them a drink.

Millie reached for a sparkling water and could feel several eyes upon them. Nic was both commanding and breathtakingly handsome in his captain's uniform.

A trio of guests approached, making small talk with the couple.

Edward and Annabel Ponsford wandered over. "Hello, Millie, Captain Armati. You both look smashing this evening."

"Thank you. We had a few hours off and thought we would drop by." Millie's eyes scanned the room as she chatted. It was a spacious suite with a large lounge, a dining area, and even a well-appointed kitchen.

Floor-to-ceiling sliders lined the wall leading out to a generous balcony. "My goodness. Is there a hot tub on the balcony?" Millie had been inside a junior suite once, but it was nothing like this.

"Yes. Harry and Kate are spoilt by all this luxury. I think this will be their last social event for a while, now that they're being forced to cut back."

"Forced to cut back?" Millie asked.

"Annabel." Edward peered down at his wife. "You know how I detest gossip."

"It's not gossip. You know it's true." Annabel turned up her nose before changing the subject. "I'm sure the captain's apartment is equally as spacious."

"It might be comparable in square footage, but it doesn't have a balcony this size, nor does it have a hot tub," Nic said. "We save the best for our guests."

"Spoken like a true company spokesman," Edward said. "The Moxeys know how to throw a party."

A few of the faces looked familiar, including the Ellises. Notably absent was Thomas Windsor.

Nic smiled politely, and Millie knew he was counting the minutes until they could leave. "Are you enjoying our voyage?"

"It's splendid. Annabel and I prefer the longer cruises with a lot of sea days. It's very relaxing."

"We noticed a cooking class pop up on the schedule this evening," Annabel said. "We lucked out and secured the last two spots."

Millie told them it was something new they were trying and she would be on hand to help host.

The Moxeys attempted to join them, but a small crowd had gathered around Nic and Millie, making it nearly impossible for anyone else to get close.

Finally, the crowd drifted away, and they were alone. "See how popular you are?" Millie teased. "We should attend these events more often."

"Over my dead body."

"Millie." Millie felt a light tap and turned to find Kate and Harry Moxey standing behind them.

"We're honored that you were able to join us for our party." Harry shook Nic's hand.

"I work most evenings, and have very little time off," Nic explained. "We can't stay long. Millie and I are covering evening shifts."

"We're glad you could make it." Kate placed a light hand on her husband's arm. "The bartenders sent by Celebrations are fabulous. They're very prompt and efficient."

"Your suite is lovely," Millie said. "I hate to be a bother, but I was wondering if I could use the restroom."

"Of course. There's a half bath tucked in behind the living room." Kate pointed in the general direction.

"Hurry back." Nic's eyes narrowed as he shot his wife a warning look.

It took her a few minutes to make it to the bathroom after being stopped several times by guests. She stepped inside the compact space and her heart sank. There was a small linen cabinet above the toilet. Other than that, the room was empty.

Millie took care of business and slipped back into the living room. Kate and Harry still had Nic cornered. Their backs were to her.

She cast a furtive glance around and made the split-second decision to take a wrong turn, stepping into the adjoining room, which happened to be the bedroom.

It was lovely and spacious, with soft gray walls. Matching nightstands were tucked inside the cutouts, and custom mirrors ran from ceiling to countertop. Recessed lighting cast the room in a warm glow. The king-size bed sported a plush down comforter. Color-coordinated pillows in the same shade of gray lined the head of the bed. A matching gray runner ran along the end.

Classical music played in the background, and Millie caught a whiff of lavender lingering in the air. She backed out of the room and ducked behind a couple who were standing near the balcony sliders.

Millie had almost made it back to Nic's side when Hilda Ellis appeared, blocking her path. "Millie Armati. What are you doing here?" she rudely asked.

"The Moxeys invited Nic to the party, so he and I decided to stop by."

"That's right. Your husband is the ship's captain. Must be nice to land not only a primo job on a cruise ship but snag the most eligible man on board."

Millie smiled, refusing to take the bait. "You're right. I am one lucky woman."

"I noticed more of the ship's security making their rounds. I'm glad they finally listened to me and are spending more time patrolling the ship."

"Our ship's security staff is always around, not to mention there are cameras in almost all public areas of the ship."

Bruce, who was standing right behind his wife, spoke. "After Hilda mentioned the incidents, I have been noticing the cameras. They're in the hallways, elevators, restaurants, you name it."

"What about the cabins?" Hilda asked. "I would think placing cameras in passengers' cabins would be viewed as an invasion of privacy."

"There are no cameras in passengers' cabins."

"I dunno." Hilda elbowed her husband. "We should check ours to make sure. I've read stories about how they put cameras on top of mirrors or behind them to spy on people."

Millie could feel the tips of her ears burn as she remembered having done the exact same thing on more than one occasion, but for good reason. "I'm sure there are no cameras in your cabin."

"It's time for us to go." Bruce consulted his watch. "I need to stop by the cabin before I head up to the casino."

"The party is just getting started," Hilda whined.

"Then, you stay. I'm leaving." Bruce lumbered off as his wife made an unhappy sound.

"At least he made the effort to join us."

"I practically had to drag him here."

Millie excused herself and joined her husband, their hosts, and another couple. As she drew closer, she noted the annoyed expression on her husband's face. "There you are."

"I'm sorry. I got sidetracked." Millie slid her arm through his. "I'm sure you're ready to head home."

"You're leaving already? Your husband is incredibly magnetic." Kate let out a low growl. "Harry and I would love for you to come back for our after-party party. It's a chance to get to know each other if you know what I mean."

"Yes. Well." Millie kept a firm grip on Nic's arm as she began backing toward the door. "We stay very busy and don't have time for a lot of extra-curricular activities."

Thankfully, another couple approached. Seizing the opportunity, Millie nearly dragged her husband out of the suite.

Nic's expression was emotionless as they strolled to the end of the hallway and then took the stairs down to the bridge. He gave the bridge captains a curt nod, never slowing until they reached their apartment.

He held the door for his wife, nearly slamming it shut as she stepped inside. "What was that?"

"What was what?" Millie swallowed hard.

"Those two. The Moxeys. While you were gone, they propositioned me multiple times about staying for their clothing-optional after-party."

"I hope you told them no."

"Told them no?" Nic roared. "They're swappers or swingers or whatever you want to call them."

Millie chewed her lower lip. "I did kind of wonder why they liked to attend the singles events. Believe me, I would have warned you had I known."

Millie watched as Nic sucked in a breath. He shrugged off his jacket and began loosening his tie. A slow smile etched his face and then his shoulders shook as he began laughing. "I do believe you've topped your own antics."

"What is that supposed to mean?"

"By convincing me to attend a swinger's party."

Millie stomped her foot. "I certainly didn't do it intentionally."

Nic was still laughing as he kicked off his shoes. "I could've gotten you back."

"How so?"

"By accepting their invitation."

"You wouldn't."

"Don't think so? It might have been worth it to teach you a lesson. I would've let you squirm for a while, thinking we were staying." Nic smiled smugly. "I'll pay you back, Millie Armati. Mark my words."

Millie covered her mouth. "You should've seen the look on your face."

"What am I going to do with you?" Nic grabbed Millie's arm and pulled her close.

"I don't know. I am sorry. I had no idea they were going to proposition you."

"Proposition us," Nic corrected. "And now that we're home and alone, I think it's time for a private party for two."

Chapter 19

Millie's first thought when she woke early the next morning was about her new schedule and what time she needed to report to guest services.

Nic, who wasn't scheduled to report to the bridge until noon, noted the glum expression on his wife's face when she joined him for breakfast. "What's wrong?"

"My first round of punishment begins this morning."

"Working at guest services."

"Yep." Millie dumped dry cereal into her bowl and added milk. "I would rather clean toilets."

"Seriously?" Nic chuckled.

"No, but it's close." Millie grabbed a spoon and plopped down in the chair. "How do I get myself into these messes?"

"By not minding your own business." Nic sobered. "Seriously, be careful today. I still don't know what to think about the note and the fact someone may have followed you into the stairwell."

"Me either. At least I'm out in the public ninety-nine percent of the time."

"It's the other one percent we need to worry about. Since I have some time off this morning, Scout and I are going to head up to the golf center. The maintenance department has just completed some renovations and I'm eager to see what they've done."

"If you run out of things to do, you can stop by guest services and make fun of me."

"You're a tough cookie. You'll be fine." Nic squeezed his wife's hand.

After breakfast, Millie stopped by Andy's office to check in and then hosted her first event before heading to guest services. Nikki was behind the desk and watched as Millie circled around to the back. "Are you really working here today?"

"I am. I got caught doing something I shouldn't have, and this is one of my punishments."

"It's not that bad. Seriously, your shift will be over before you know it." Nikki gave her some brief instructions on running the various software programs, which were similar to those Millie was already familiar with. The only one she struggled with was the customer complaints or comments screen. It took a few practice runs before Millie had it down.

"You can work here." Nikki placed her at the station on the end and then motioned to the woman who was next in line.

Millie smiled as she greeted her. "Hello. How can I help you?"

"I've misplaced my keycard."

"We'll be happy to issue you a new one."

Nikki showed Millie how to print new keycards and then walked her through the steps on how to disable the old one. "You always want to disable the lost one."

"In case it's found by another passenger and they try to charge items to it," Millie guessed.

"Bingo."

Millie finished the task and handed the woman her new card.

"Thank you. It won't happen again. I'm running upstairs to the gift shop to buy a lanyard so I can hang it around my neck."

The woman left, and Millie motioned for a couple waiting in line. They placed a beach bag on the counter. "We found this on the pool deck. Can we leave it with you?"

"You can." Millie began entering the information in the system, which would enable others working in guest services to locate the item if someone reported it missing. "Pink bag, blue waves with a flamingo on the side."

"It's been sitting on one of the pool loungers for a few hours. Either someone forgot about it or they were saving the chair."

Millie's head shot up. "Did you happen to notice if a crewmember was on hand collecting unclaimed items?"

"No, ma'am."

Millie thanked the couple and then gave Andy a quick call.

"Hello, Millie. Having fun?"

"Yes, more fun than I deserve," she said sarcastically. "Two passengers turned in a beach bag they claim was left on a pool deck lounger for a few hours. You might want to send someone upstairs to start clearing the chairs."

279

"I'm on it."

Millie ended the call and then began rummaging through the bag. There was no form of identification, so she placed it in the nearby lost and found closet.

A familiar face appeared. It was Thomas Windsor. "Millie Armati. What are you doing here?"

"Working." Millie mumbled a vague excuse. "Can I help you with something?"

"Yes. It appears a questionable charge has popped up on my folio." Thomas handed Millie his cell phone, displaying a list of items charged to his account. "It's the most recent one."

Millie slipped her reading glasses on. "The spa charged you for a bikini wax."

"I left my bikini at home," Thomas quipped.

"I'm sure you did," Millie chuckled, as she reached for her mouse. "Is there anything else that looks off?"

"Nope. We missed you at the Mix and Mingle Singles party yesterday."

"And I missed you at the Moxey's evening cocktail party last night." Millie finished issuing the credit and handed Thomas a receipt.

"You attended the Moxey's party? I didn't peg you as that kinda gal."

"I'm not. In fact, I guess I'm a little naïve. Something always struck me as a little odd when they showed up at the singles get-togethers, but I never put two and two together."

Thomas leaned an elbow on the counter. "Let me guess...one of them propositioned you."

"Nic," Millie grinned. "They're nice enough folks, just not my type, if you know what I mean."

"I certainly do. Are you hosting this afternoon's singles party?"

Millie consulted her app and scrolled through the screen. "As a matter of fact, I am. I'll see you later?"

"You will." After Thomas left, Millie motioned for the next person in line to join her. The hours flew by and she was surprised when her scheduler app went off, letting her know her shift had ended. "I'm heading out," she whispered in Nikki's ear.

"See? It wasn't so bad."

"You're right. I'll see you tomorrow, same time." Millie hustled to her hosting event and was wrapping up her morning routine when Patterson radioed, asking her to meet him in his office.

"Your timing is impeccable. I'm on my way." She arrived to find not only Patterson, but Nic, Donovan, and Suharto there, as well.

Millie said the first thing that popped into her head. "I didn't do it."

"Come in, Millie."

"What is going on?" Her eyes traveled around the room, and her gut told her something was wrong.

"I'm assigning you a guard."

"Assigning me a guard?"

"I've also placed the ship's security team on high alert." Patterson shifted his computer monitor and motioned for the others to gather around. "It appears the strangler may have claimed his next victim."

Millie studied the grainy image on the screen and noticed it was near the ship's helipad. A person, their back to the surveillance camera, dragged a bulky object to the center of the helipad and then dropped it on the "H."

Keeping their head down and obscuring their image, the person scurried off. Millie noted the time stamp—one forty-five a.m.

"When did the crew find the victim?" Nic asked.

"Around three this morning. As you know, the helipad is in an isolated area of the ship, not even known about by most passengers," Patterson said. "We're reviewing every camera footage, every deck, but this could take days and then we might not find anything. We've sent a report to the Southampton authorities to see if this matches the strangler's method of operating."

Millie felt lightheaded. "The strangler killed someone on board the ship and dumped their body on the helipad."

"I want round-the-clock security for Millie until the ship docks in Miami," Nic said.

"Already done. Since Suharto is in charge of the gangway and we're not stopping until we reach Bermuda, he'll be with Millie at all times."

Patterson continued. "We've been keeping an eye on the passengers linked to Clarissa Sinclair. I'm starting to suspect we're focusing our attention on the wrong suspects." Frustrated, Patterson abruptly stood. "I'm at a loss. We can't follow every single passenger around this ship."

"We have limited resources, and the strangler knows it," Donovan said. "It's not like we can stop off at the nearest port and call in reinforcements."

Donovan had a point. They were in the middle of the Atlantic Ocean, miles away from land.

"The note I received said 'you're next,' so either the strangler is throwing out false information or had a change of plans," Millie pointed out.

"It could be either or," Patterson said.

"A lot can happen in the next three days, before we reach Bermuda," Donovan said.

"I trust you to do whatever is necessary to keep both the passengers and crew on board this ship as safe as possible." Nic stepped back. "I need to head back to the bridge but would like an update as soon as you're able to get confirmation about whether this person was another strangler victim."

"Hold up." Millie lifted a hand. "Whose body was found? Was it a passenger or a crewmember?"

Patterson told her the victim's name. "And now you know why Suharto will be with you from here on out."

Chapter 20

"Hilda Ellis is dead," Millie whispered.

"Her husband, Bruce, who returned to his cabin after closing down the casino, found her missing and called security." Patterson told them as soon as he reported her missing, every available security guard began searching for her. "And that's when her body was discovered on the helipad."

"Maybe he did it," Millie said.

"His alibi checks out. The keycard notifications match up to what he told us. The last video surveillance we have of Hilda is at eleven-thirty last night. She stopped by the pizza place to grab a couple slices of pizza and then the beverage station, where she fixed a cup of tea. We traced her as far as deck six and that's the last image we have of her, at least as far as we know."

"So, between eleven-thirty and...when was the last image of her captured?"

"Fifteen minutes later."

Millie pressed her palms together. "Hilda grabs pizza and then fixes a cup of tea. Less than three hours later, the killer is caught on camera dragging her body to the helipad."

"Correct. We've already checked every possible surveillance recording, not only on the connecting decks, but everywhere in between. It's as if Hilda vanished into thin air and somewhere along the way, ran into her killer."

"What about the couple's cabin?" Donovan asked. "Was anything disturbed? Any indication of trouble?"

"Nothing. Nada. Zip. Mr. Ellis is cooperating. He's given us access to everything." Patterson's cell phone chimed. "Corporate is calling."

Suharto and Millie quietly made their way out of the office, leaving Patterson, Nic, and Donovan behind.

"I'm sorry you got stuck with me," Millie apologized.

"I am not stuck with you, Miss Millie. I am looking forward to what we will do."

"I can promise you one thing, we won't be getting into any trouble."

They began making their way to the end of the corridor. "I'm still on break and starving. Are you hungry?"

"I am always hungry."

"Good. Let's swing by the grill to grab a bite to eat."

The pool area was packed. Now that the ship was cruising south and to a warmer climate, the passengers were taking advantage of the balmy weather and plentiful sunshine. The mood was lighter and the skies brighter.

Andy had even thought to update the live music to calypso tunes, and the melodic sounds of steel drums wafted in the air.

"It is busy up here," Suharto said.

"It is," she agreed. "I don't know about you, but I'm looking forward to more tropical temperatures."

"Me too."

Millie stepped up to the poolside grill and placed a hot dog on her plate. She added a slice of dill pickle, two scoops of sweet relish, a generous helping of spicy mustard and a spoonful of chopped red onion. The potato salad looked nice and creamy, so she added a scoop of that, along with coleslaw. A handful of potato chips took up the last corner of real estate on her plate.

With a stop for some iced tea, Millie waited for Suharto to load up his plate before finding a shady table for two in the corner.

Millie prayed over her food, adding a special prayer for Hilda Ellis and her husband, Bruce, before lifting her head. She found Suharto watching her. "You are a Christian," he said.

"I am." Millie glanced at Suharto's tag, listing his home country as Indonesia. "Your country is mostly Muslim."

"Yes. But we also have many Christians," he replied in a clipped voice. "It is a good country. My home."

"And warm."

"For most of the year. We do not get cold. I did not like the British Isles. It is pretty and green but too cold for my blood."

"Mine too," Millie said. "Although I spent most of my life in Michigan where the winter months are cold and snowy."

"I have never seen snow."

"It's like rain except it freezes and it's not fun to drive on."

"I will take your word for it." Suharto took a big bite of his cheeseburger, loaded with toppings. A glob of catsup oozed out and landed on a French fry. "The food is much better up here. I think I will like working with you for the duration of our voyage."

"It will give us a chance to get to know each other better." Millie spread a forkful of coleslaw along the top of her hotdog. "What was your favorite part of the British Isles?"

"I was able to get off in Invergordon, when Siren of the Seas was waiting for you, the captain and the others to catch up after you were left behind in Orkney."

"Don't remind me."

Suharto's smile widened. "I have worked on this ship for many years. The most exciting have been since you joined us, Miss Millie."

Millie thought about all the incidents that had occurred, the ship being hijacked, her ex-husband's soon-to-be wife being murdered, Scout's dognapping, the ship's officers being poisoned. Yes, there had been some exciting events since Millie joined Siren of the Seas. "And some of it I could do without."

While they ate, they chatted about life on board the ship, and Suharto entertained Millie with stories about mishaps at the gangway, most involving passengers who had lost track of time and were almost left behind.

"What is the most outrageous reason someone has ever given you for not making it back to the ship on time?" Millie asked.

Suharto grew quiet as he thought about it. "The handcuffs."

"Handcuffs?"

"A passenger returned to the ship handcuffed to a potted plant. Since produce and live plants from the islands are not allowed, she had to empty the pot before boarding the ship."

Millie chuckled. "Why on earth was she handcuffed to a potted plant?"

"She was drinking at a local bar, and I think her friend made a bet."

"Let me guess. It happened in Cozumel."

"Yes. I have many funny Cozumel port stories. Remind me to tell you about the monkey sometime."

"I will." Millie and Suharto made it to the theater with a few minutes to spare.

Suharto stayed close by, behind the stage's curtains while she and Alison Coulter, one of the ship's dancers, hosted several rounds of bingo.

The women also co-hosted a ballroom dancing class, and Millie talked Suharto into joining her on the dance floor. He easily picked up the steps, and soon they were whirling their way around the floor.

Their next stop was The Vines. Annette and Amit were already there and setting up for the cooking class.

Her friend did a double take when she spotted Suharto. "Hey, guys. What's up Suharto?"

"I am accompanying Millie for the rest of our voyage."

Annette tilted her head. "You're accompanying Millie?"

"Yes, because of the passenger's death."

"I heard there was a death but didn't catch the name or details."

Millie briefly filled her in. "Patterson and Nic are concerned that I'm the next target."

"So, they believe the strangler is on board the ship."

"Last I heard, Patterson is waiting for confirmation from the UK authorities to see if there's a match."

"I still don't understand why you're a target, Millie. Sure, you like to stick your nose in where it doesn't belong, but the strangler wouldn't know that."

"Your guess is as good as mine. The only possible link I can think of is the port and Halbert. It could be the strangler believes I know something and has set his or her sights on me."

"I have been thinking about it, too," Suharto said. "You spent many days visiting Halbert when the ship was in port. Perhaps you caught a glimpse of the strangler and he now views you as a possible witness."

"I suppose. I mean, he made a point of going back and killing Edith Branson after all these years.

Perhaps he considered her a loose end and me the same." Millie rubbed her hands together, eyeing the table Amit was setting up for the cooking demonstration. "What's on the menu?"

"Healthy is the theme. I'm making chicken kabobs, Greek salad, homemade tzatziki, a dipping sauce for the kabobs and Milopita."

"Milopita."

"It's a Greek apple upside-down cake." Annette shifted her gaze, glancing over Millie's shoulder. "Our guests are arriving."

Millie hustled to the door and began escorting the attendees to their seats, which were arranged in a semi-circle around the cooking stations.

Annette waited until the last person had arrived to greet them. She talked about the dishes as she assembled the Greek salad first. After she finished, Millie began spooning the salad into tasting dishes and handed one to each of the attendees.

Up next were the chicken kabobs, consisting of chunks of chicken breast, layers of bell pepper, zucchini, cherry tomatoes, red onion and sliced mushrooms cooked on a skewer. Annette used an indoor grill for cooking and prepared enough so that each participant could sample one kabob.

Even though Millie had already eaten, the smell of the grilling meat made her mouth water. Since she had made extras, Annette shared the tasty dish with her assistants, as well as Suharto.

Millie added a generous scoop of tzatziki to her plate and dipped her chicken in the creamy mix. "This is delicious," she said.

Annette waited for Millie and Amit to collect the dirty dishes before giving them step-by-step instructions on making the Milopita as she drizzled warm brown sugar sauce over the top of the finished dessert.

Once again, Millie passed out the tasty dessert treats, and then she and the others sampled a piece.

The tart green apples gave it a hint of tang, which was tempered by the sweet sauce.

While Millie and Amit cleaned up, Annette answered questions. The first few were specific to the recipes and then they became more general—about food consumption on board the ship and the inner workings of the galley.

At precisely one hour and thirty-five minutes, Annette's culinary presentation ended. The attendees stopped by to thank her and her co-hosts. Several remarked on how they wished there were more classes available.

"The food was delicious," one attendee gushed. "I should book the specialty restaurant, at least for one meal."

"Hold on." Millie darted to her backpack and pulled out the stack of discount coupons Andy had given her. "We're offering discounts for attending the cooking class." She handed the woman three coupons and then hurried off to catch the others.

The last person left, and Millie closed the door behind her before joining her friends. "I call this a huge success."

"It was fun." Amit nodded. "I don't get a chance to talk to passengers unless I'm delivering room service."

"And the food was delicious." Suharto patted his stomach. "I could get used to hanging out with Millie."

"Be prepared to get into trouble." Annette placed the dirty dishes on her cart. "The fun and games are over. It's time to head back to the real world, my friends."

After they left, Millie consulted her app. Up next was a VIP spa event. It was the one event her new sidekick didn't appear to enjoy. Poor Suharto looked uncomfortable as he sat in a dryer chair, flipping through a fashion magazine while waiting for Millie to finish.

Finally, Camille, the spa's manager, pulled Millie aside. "What's up with the security guy?"

"I recently received a vague threat. Patterson and some of the other staff thought it would be best to have security keep an eye on me until we reach Miami."

"Does it have anything to do with the dead woman?"

"Yeah." Millie lowered her voice as a spa employee escorted a passenger to the counter to pay for her services. "The woman claims someone was following her around the ship. The same happened to me, and then I received a disturbing anonymous note."

"The buzz we've heard is they think the strangler is on board. I've heard it from both staff and passengers," Camille said, "and I've noticed beefed up security everywhere."

"It's a concern."

Millie finished the event, and then she and Suharto headed out. "It's break time. If you want to walk me back to the apartment, I'll stay there until my shift picks up again for the Mix and Mingle Singles event at five in the Paradise Lounge."

"I will stay with you, Miss Millie. It is my job."

"You're the boss." It was a quick trip from the spa to the apartment. Nic was on the bridge with another of the newer staff captains. He gave Millie and Suharto a nod as they passed by.

Scout greeted them at the door. Thrilled to have company, he barely acknowledged Millie's presence and began circling Suharto's legs.

Suharto gently picked the small pup up. Scout promptly pawed at his chin and licked his hand.

"You've made a new friend," Millie teased.

"He is a good dog."

"You can open the slider and let him out."

While Suharto carried the pup onto the balcony, Millie kicked her shoes off and turned their home computer on. She checked her emails and answered one from her daughter, Beth, before opening a new search screen.

Curious to find out what the Southampton news was reporting and if there was an update on the strangler, she typed in Southampton Strangler. There was one new story, published less than an hour ago.

Millie clicked on the link, her breath catching in her throat when she read the headline.

Chapter 21

"What is it?" Suharto leaned in as Millie read aloud the first sentence of the news story. "The Southampton authorities received information from officers on board mega cruise liner, Siren of the Seas, and believe a new strangler victim has been identified. The liner, which spent the summer based out of Southampton for the British Isles itinerary, departed five days ago to return to its home port in Miami, Florida."

The story didn't identify the victim, pending notification of family, but said the victim was traveling with a group and the body would be flown back to the UK upon arrival in Bermuda.

"The passengers, they will hear about this," Suharto predicted.

"I'm sure they will." Millie did a mental calculation. They were still five days away from reaching Bermuda. "A lot can happen in five days."

She grabbed her cell phone and began scrolling through her messages until she reached the one Hilda had sent her, insisting she had caught her stalker on camera.

"What is that?" Suharto asked.

"Hilda sent me a picture she'd snapped. She was certain she'd caught the person who was following her on camera." Millie tapped the screen to make it bigger. "It's still too small. I'll forward it to my laptop." With a few quick clicks, the message was sent. She downloaded and then enlarged it.

Suharto studied the image. "When was this taken?"

"Tuesday evening. Hilda showed it to me Wednesday. I forgot all about it until now." Millie told him how Hilda had grabbed some pizza and was on her way back to the cabin when she got the feeling someone was following her. "She was a creature of habit, making the pizza station one of her regular stops."

"This is near the Teen Scene on deck nine. The pizza station is on deck eleven. Hilda and her husband's cabin is on deck four."

"Correct. Why would Hilda grab pizza and go to the other end of the ship on a completely different deck? I guess I should've asked her." Millie continued studying the photo. "I'm sure Patterson and the security department checked the surveillance cameras in this area."

"Yes. I believe I remember Ms. Ellis reporting the incident and Patterson checking the cameras."

Millie shifted so that she faced Suharto. "I know some serial killers randomly select their victims, but I think the strangler specifically picked the women that he or she did. There's a connection, but what? I need to do a little more digging around."

"I will help." Suharto carried a chair from the dining room to the desk. "We will search for clues."

"Let's start with Edith Branson." Millie pulled up several stories, pointing out anything she thought might be a clue.

Up next was the woman from the local uni, Sophie Young. "This was such a tragic death. What a promising future this woman had. I'm sure her father, a barrister, would love to get his hands on the strangler." Millie started exiting the screen before realizing she'd almost missed the last sentence. "Ms. Young worked alongside her father at his firm and was obtaining a postgraduate degree."

The third victim's name was being withheld, and Millie wondered why. It was the female jogger whose body was found in the park, her faithful pup guarding her body.

Millie read the story aloud. "This is interesting. The unnamed female was part of a jury some years back and claimed she felt she was being stalked after the trial."

"Does it say what sort of trial?"

"No." Millie picked Scout up. "It's almost as if it was an afterthought, but enough to comment on."

"Is there any way to link the university student and the juror?" Suharto asked.

"You read my mind." Millie clicked back to Sophie Young's story. "Her father's name is Arthur Young. He's a barrister in Southern England."

Millie attempted several searches of Arthur Young's cases, but hit a dead end with every angle she tried. "We're chasing our tails and going in circles."

"There was another victim, Clarissa Sinclair," Suharto reminded her.

"Yes. She was apparently onto something about the strangler. Let's see what we can find out about her." Millie hit the jackpot and found page after page of stories about Clarissa's rather brief journalistic career.

What Millie gleaned from all the glowing reports was the woman was a crackpot at solving cold cases. Unfortunately, it appeared the final one cost Clarissa her life. "I'm sure the authorities are focusing their attention on tracking her steps during the days and hours leading up to her death."

Millie studied the notes Suharto had taken on Edith Branson. "Edith's husband founded a company and died decades ago, leaving her a wealthy woman. Why would the strangler target her?"

"Or any of them," Suharto said.

"Wealthy widow, university student, jogger and crackpot reporter."

"And now Hilda Ellis."

"Right. The only thing they have in common is they were all female."

"You have very fast internet."

"We do. I'm not sure if the internet gurus gave us some super speedy device, but it's certainly faster than those dinosaurs downstairs in the crewmember's lounge."

"The computers are very slow. It is hard to use minutes to contact my family back home. My son, Bagus, just turned five." Suharto's eyes lit. "He is a busy boy. I tried to get through to my family yesterday, but since we left Southampton, the reception, it is not good. We are so far out."

Millie tightened her grip on Scout and slid out of the chair. "We still have some time before our next event. Why don't you use our computer?"

"Use your computer?"

"Yes. I would love to see pictures of your family."

"Th-thank you, Miss Millie." Suharto reached for the mouse, and then paused. "Are you sure?"

"Positive. You should get some sort of perk for putting up with me," she joked.

"You are too kind." Suharto opened a new search screen and then accessed his email account. There were several messages from his parents and his wife. One from Suharto's wife included pictures of her holding their son. Along with the photos was a video of the smiling baby and wife blowing kisses.

At one point, his wife's lip trembled, and Millie could feel tears burn the back of her eyes. "It must be hard being so far from home."

"Sometimes...I miss them so much, but Siren of the Seas, the people I work with, they are my family too."

Millie snuggled Scout. "I feel the same way."

Suharto gazed longingly at his family, and a thought popped into Millie's head. "Would you like to make a video to send back?"

"I have tried before, but it is so slow. The videos, they do not load."

Millie waved her cell phone in the air. "We can use my phone or your phone. Once we record it, we'll send it to your email and then you can forward it to your family."

"Thank you, Millie. My phone, it works fine. The problem is sending it."

Millie gave Suharto a few minutes to figure out what he wanted to say. When he was ready, she started recording and then decided it was too dark, so they stepped out onto the balcony.

Scout followed behind to investigate. "Bagus, he loves animals. Do you mind if I showed him Scout?"

"Of course, not."

Millie started over. At first, Suharto was a little stiff and robotic as he told his wife Siren of the Seas was journeying back to Miami. Scout seemed to loosen him up.

"This is Scout, Captain Armati and Miss Millie's pup." Suharto grasped Scout's paw and began waving it. "Scout says 'hi', Bagus."

"In case you are wondering. Mr. Patterson has put me in charge of guarding the captain's wife, who is also the ship's assistant cruise director." Suharto paused and Millie turned the phone for a quick shot of her smiling. She waved before focusing back in on Suharto.

"Thank you for the video of you and Bagus. Millie allowed me to use her laptop so I could send this video. With all my love." Suharto blew a kiss at the camera.

Millie tapped the screen to stop recording. "This should be short enough so it won't give us too much trouble uploading."

They returned inside, and Millie watched as Suharto accessed the file. With a few clicks, he attached the video and pressed the send button.

It spun for a few seconds and then disappeared. "It has gone," Suharto said. "Like magic."

"You can use the computer while you're here." Millie glanced around. "Since you'll be staying with the captain and me, I hope you don't mind sleeping on the sofa. It pulls out into a bed."

"It will be fine. I will sleep on the floor if I have to."

"That won't be necessary. You can put your things in the linen closet in the downstairs bathroom and feel free to use any of the soaps and shampoos in the storage closet." Touched by Suharto's loyalty to not only Siren of the Seas, but his family, Millie made a mental note to do something nice for him before his guarding duties ended.

In the meantime, they needed to head out to the Paradise Lounge to host the singles party.

Thomas Windsor was there. The Moxeys never showed, and she could only imagine how shocked

314

the group was that another of their traveling companions had been murdered. During the brief moments Millie was alone, she thought about the strangler's victims.

There had to be a link other than all of them being female. Hilda had been convinced she was being followed. Millie wondered how her husband, Bruce, was holding up.

He'd struck Millie as slightly standoffish, but then Hilda had been over the top, never afraid to voice her opinion or speak out. While Hilda had been more social, her husband preferred to spend his time in the casino.

From her brief conversations with the woman, she knew that she made her rounds around the ship, usually alone. Millie reminded herself to catch up with the Ponsfords and the Moxeys to express her condolences.

Suharto hung back and watched the festivities from the sidelines. They moved from event to event, and it was a whirlwind of activities.

By the time it was their dinner hour, Suharto and Millie were starving. "Let's head downstairs."

The crew dining room was packed, and they joined the long line. They filled their plates and circled the room, finally giving up trying to find empty chairs, so they wandered down the hall to the crewmember's lounge.

A trio was seated at the bar, and two others were near the back playing pool. The lounge chairs were open, and Millie and Suharto settled in at a small table off to the side. While they ate, they discussed their day, and then Millie asked Suharto to name his favorite part of his job.

He thought about it for a minute. "The people. I am a people person. They do such funny things. Most, they are very nice. They make up for the unhappy ones."

"Speaking of unhappy passengers, I have guest services desk duty tomorrow."

"Because you were caught in Mr. Windsor's cabin."

"By the big man himself." Millie stabbed a meatball and swirled it in the spaghetti sauce. "I'm convinced Patterson has super senses and can sniff out bad behavior."

"He is very smart."

"Almost too smart," Millie joked. "You would think I would learn by now to keep my nose clean and stay off the radar."

"You cannot." Suharto tapped the side of his forehead. "Your mind, it is always working. I watch you and I can see you are very observant."

"I'll take that as a compliment. Thank you."

A woman walked in, carrying a tray of food. She hovered near the door as she looked around. It was the new server, Joy, that she and the captain had met at the beginning of the journey. Millie caught her eye and waved her over. "Hi, Joy."

"Hello, Millie. The crew dining room is packed."

"It is. Would you like to join us?"

"Sure."

Millie waited for Joy to set her tray on the table and slide into an empty seat before making the introductions. "Are you still enjoying your job?"

"I love it. I love people and people watching. They're so interesting and a cruise ship is the perfect spot to learn about other cultures."

While Joy ate, Millie asked her about her recent travels and her favorite places. She was impressed with the woman's adventurous spirit, not afraid to travel alone and meet new people.

After finishing their food, Millie and Suharto parted ways with Joy. They swung by the galley to chat with Annette. Since she was up to her eyeballs in meal preparations, they kept moving.

Although the gift shop was open, it was empty, except for Cat, who was standing in the back. "Let's pop in and chat with Cat."

Millie led the way to the back.

"Hey, Millie. Suharto. I heard you had security detail since that poor woman's body was found this morning."

"Yes, and I'm happy for the company. We're on our dinner break and were passing by so we thought we would pop in and say 'hi.'" Millie pointed to the arrangement of flowers on the counter. "Did Andy send you flowers?"

"No, but he stopped by a short time ago when he was on break. The flowers are for the Ponsfords and the Moxeys. Donovan wanted to send flowers as a token of sympathy for the death of Hilda Ellis."

"What about Hilda's husband?"

"His ginormous bouquet was already delivered by Pastor Evans. Donovan thought having the pastor speak with him was a good idea. I'm waiting for my help to show up so someone can deliver these."

"Suharto and I can deliver them since I planned to offer my condolences, as well."

"That would be great." Cat slid the glass vases across the counter. "Their names and cabin numbers are on the front of the card."

"I've been to the Moxey's suite. It's close to the Ponsford's balcony cabin." Millie took a quick glance and then handed one of the bouquets to Suharto. "We're on it."

"Thanks, Millie, and stay safe. This whole strangler thing has me on pins and needles."

"I will make sure Miss Millie is safe," Suharto promised.

They made their way into the corridor and crossed to the other end of the ship for the trek up to the Moxey's suite.

The door was ajar, and Millie gave it a light rap.

Kate Moxey answered moments later. Her eyes were red and her complexion pale. "Hello, Millie."

"Hello, Kate. I'm—we're sorry to bother you. The captain and crew wish to extend their condolences." Millie held out the bouquet of flowers.

"That's very thoughtful. Captain Armati, as well as several of the other ship's captains, have stopped by to offer the same." Kate took the bouquet and eased the door open. "I can't believe Hilda is gone. First Clarissa and now Hilda."

Millie caught a glimpse of Harry and the Ponsfords, who were inside the suite and seated on the settee. "The other floral arrangement is for Annabel and Edward."

Kate pressed a light hand to her forehead. "Where are my manners? Please...come in."

Annabel sprang to her feet as Millie and Suharto made their way into the living room. "Millie."

"Hello, Annabel, Edward and Harry. I am so sorry to hear about Hilda's unfortunate passing."

"It's awful. Poor Bruce had to be sedated."

"I'm sure he's in shock." Millie motioned to Suharto, who held out the second floral arrangement. "The flowers are for you."

"Thank you." Annabel placed the arrangement on the coffee table.

"We can't stay. We just wanted to drop off the flowers and offer our condolences."

"The captain and staff have been very supportive and we're grateful for their concern," Harry said.

"Are you continuing on until we reach Miami?" Millie asked.

"We're disembarking in Bermuda, to accompany Bruce back to the UK," Annabel said. "Quite frankly, we're reeling from her tragic death."

"I've been wondering what Bruce will do with the holiday home he and Hilda purchased with their settlement money," Annabel said.

"I'm sure he'll sell it, since he's never even laid eyes on it. The holiday home was Hilda's idea."

Millie stared at Edward as something began percolating in the back of her mind, some small clue, some niggling of a lead.

Suharto spoke. "Mr. Patterson has increased the ship's security to Level 5, the highest security level possible."

Kate accompanied Millie and Suharto to the door. "We've been in touch with family and friends back in the UK. It's all over the news. The authorities are certain the strangler is on board this ship."

"I've heard the same," Millie admitted. "It's best we remain on guard and not venture out alone while Mr. Patterson, the ship's head of security, and his men try to track the killer down."

Kate offered them a grim smile. "They haven't been able to catch him yet. I'm not sure how successful they will be at this point."

Millie insisted they contact her if they needed anything before they made their way out of the suite.

Suharto waited until they reached the stairwell to speak. "They are very sad for their loss."

"And worried. Who can blame them?" Millie thought about the clues, about the victims, about her note and being followed. Was she next? It gave her great comfort knowing Suharto was by her side.

It wasn't until later that evening, after turning in for the night and she listened to Nic's soft snores, that Millie began putting the pieces together.

She would need to do more digging around. Unfortunately, it would have to wait until morning.

Chapter 22

Suharto was already up, the sleeper sofa back to its original position, and the sheets and blankets neatly folded when Millie made her way downstairs early the next morning. "Good morning, Suharto. How did you sleep?"

"Like a baby." Suharto tilted his head and placed his folded hands on his cheek. "It was like sleeping on a cloud."

Millie arched a brow. "Our sleeper sofa is harder than a rock."

"But you gave me so many extra blankets, it was nice."

"Nic is upstairs getting ready. Would you care for some coffee?"

"Yes, please." Suharto followed Millie into the kitchen. "I hope you don't mind, but Scout wanted to go out."

"Not at all. Thank you."

"You are welcome. What is our day like today?"

"Busy," Millie said. "I didn't sleep well. I couldn't stop thinking about all the clues. Something Annabel Ponsford said yesterday stuck with me." She told him what it was. "I think I'm onto something and now it's all a matter of unraveling the mystery."

"It is dangerous."

"Yes, and I believe my life is also in danger. Hilda inadvertently put it in danger when she sent me that picture of her stalker." Millie's eyes grew round as saucers. "That's it." She hustled past Suharto and hurried to the computer.

Millie's hand trembled as she grabbed the yellow pad and studied the notes Suharto had taken. It all began with the first victim the strangler targeted during his second round of killings—Edith Branson.

Suharto joined her, peering over her shoulder as she began listing the clues. One by one they all tumbled out and onto the paper. Clue by clue. It was almost as if Clarissa Sinclair was there, whispering the secrets in Millie's ear.

The only mystery left now was how the strangler discovered Clarissa had uncovered his identity. Only she and the killer could answer that question.

She scoured the internet, searching for information about the strangler's first killings from several years back. Millie jotted their names down and began comparing them to the victims from the past few months. Unable to find a link, she finally gave up. "I need to get this down to Patterson."

"He does not start his shift for another half an hour," Suharto said.

"We'll grab a bite to eat while we wait." Millie ran upstairs to tell Nic they were leaving.

Suharto was waiting at the bottom of the stairs when she returned. "You can ask the others who were traveling with Ms. Sinclair."

"No. I think it would be a mistake to tip my hand. If they don't believe me, they'll start talking and it could blow up in my face. There's only one way to catch the killer. We need to set a trap and lure him, or her, to the one person they still consider a threat."

"You."

"Yes. I would have to be the bait to lure the Southampton Strangler out and into the open." Millie absentmindedly stared at Suharto. "I think I gave myself the perfect setup to force the strangler's hand."

"I do not like this. Not at all. My job is to protect you. I think you need to talk to Mr. Patterson."

"I will."

Suharto and Millie were on their way downstairs to grab something to eat when Annette radioed. "Where are you?"

"Suharto and I just left the apartment."

"I'll feed you if you swing by here."

"You're twisting our arms," Millie joked. "We're on our way."

When they arrived, not only was Annette and Amit on hand, but Danielle and Cat were there too.

Suharto sniffed appreciatively. "Something smells delicious."

"Bacon. You can't go wrong with bacon." Annette pointed to the stack of fluffy pancakes, the plateful of bacon and another pan, this one filled with scrambled eggs. There was also a towering pile of buttery toast and a side of mixed fruit.

"What's the occasion?" Millie asked.

"I called an emergency breakfast meeting. We're concerned about you," Annette said. "Cat heard the ship's security is almost one hundred percent certain the strangler is on board. Patterson wouldn't have assigned Suharto to guard you unless he thought your life was in danger."

"He's right, and I believe I'm being targeted." Millie removed the sheet of paper and clues from her pocket and made her way down the list. "I still have some confirming to do, to connect the dots between Edith Branson, the first targeted victim, followed by Sophie Young. I'm sure Patterson can find out fairly quickly if those two, along with the unidentified juror, the jogger, are linked."

"Wouldn't the authorities be looking for a similar link?" Cat asked.

"Not necessarily. In fact, if I hadn't overheard an important clue, I wouldn't have, either. It was all a matter of timing."

"The swinger's cocktail party you attended ended up being a worthy endeavor?" Danielle teased.

"If my hunch is correct, it may have been the one thing that is going to trip up the strangler." Millie started to mention what Halbert and Nic had said, that the authorities believed Clarissa may have injured the strangler during her struggle.

Cat leaned in. "What were you going to say?"

"The authorities may have a way to link the strangler to the scene."

"Meaning DNA," Danielle guessed.

"Possibly. Unless he was careful enough so that there was no DNA to sample. And even if they could get a sample and a match, how long will it take to get the results? I'm sure they're prioritizing it, but even a day or two might be too long." Millie plucked a slice of bacon from the plate. "All I need to do is spread the right information to the right people and then wait for the strangler to come after me, but on my terms, not his. He makes his move and bam!" Millie slapped her palms together. "Patterson and his men can take the strangler off the streets forever."

"You've gotten yourself into some serious predicaments, but this one might top the list," Danielle said. "I hope you know what you're doing."

"I don't—at least not yet, but if I already have a target on my back, I would much rather face this head on than be looking over my shoulder for the next week."

*****

Millie and Suharto finished their breakfast and made a fast track to Patterson's office. Since Suharto knew his boss's schedule, he was correct in guessing the head of security was in his office.

There was a flicker of surprise on Patterson's face as he waved them into the room. "Problems already? Is Millie driving you crazy?"

"No, sir." Suharto grinned. "I love Millie. She's the best."

"Aw." Millie touched his arm. "You are so sweet. I feel like I have a new partner in crime."

Patterson wagged his finger. "You're not allowed to corrupt Suharto."

"He's keeping me on the straight and narrow. We're here because I've stumbled upon some clues I think might tie the strangler's victims together. If my hunch is right, I know who it is." Millie unfolded her sheet of paper and handed it to Patterson.

He studied the list, his mouth forming a grim line. "How did you put this together?"

"I'm glad you asked." Millie placed her hands behind her back. "I've been driving myself crazy, trying to figure out why I would be a target, and then it dawned on me. It wasn't so much someone following me into the stairwell, which may or may not have been a coincidence. It was the picture Hilda Ellis forwarded to me. The more I thought about it, the more the pieces began falling into place."

"How long do you think it will take for the authorities to confirm Millie's suspicions regarding the link between the strangler's victims and the suspect?" Suharto asked.

"Hours. I'm guessing they're getting heat from the powers that be and are eager to solve this case," Patterson said. "If your hunch pans out, I owe you one."

"I've already figured out how you can pay me back."

"Toss out your suspension," Patterson guessed.

"Both mine and Cat's."

"And remove you from the guest services rotation."

"Nah." Millie waved dismissively. "I actually had fun working alongside Nikki and the rest of the staff. It's good for me to hear firsthand the passengers' problems. I was thinking more along the lines of a credit toward future misdemeanors."

Patterson grimaced. "You mean the next time you exhibit a lack of judgment and stick your nose in where it doesn't belong you want me to cut you some slack?"

"Precisely."

"We'll see." Patterson promised to contact Millie as soon as he received word back, and he was already on the phone before they stepped out of his office.

"You are good." Suharto's eyes filled with admiration. "Perhaps you should consider a job in the security department."

"No way. I love working with the passengers. I'll just stick my nose in when I feel it's needed. Besides, if I'm right, I'm almost certain I've set myself up for a free pass."

It was late afternoon, almost evening, by the time Patterson radioed to let Millie know he'd heard from the Southampton authorities. "I'm holding a security department meeting in the crew member's dining room in half an hour."

"So, I was right," Millie said.

"Maybe, but there's a twist."

"C'mon. Can't you at least give me a hint?"

"I just did. See you in a few." Patterson signed off and Millie made an unhappy sound as she clipped her radio to her belt.

A minor crisis sidetracked Suharto and Millie when a passenger insisted they accompany her to the golf simulator, which was on the fritz. Millie called for maintenance and waited for them to arrive before they hustled down the side steps.

She didn't slow until she reached the crew deck. Suharto wasn't far behind, struggling to catch his breath. "You are too fast, Miss Millie."

"Sorry. I forgot you were behind me." Millie propelled him down the hallway to the dining room. The place was packed, and the only spot they were able to squeeze into was in the corner.

Millie bounced onto the tips of her toes, but she wasn't able to see a thing. She finally gave up and climbed onto a chair.

Nic, along with Donovan, Andy and Kimel Pang, the head of housekeeping, stood near the front of the room.

Patterson caught Millie's eye and gave a small nod of his head. "Thank you for dropping what you were doing and coming down here for this important meeting. As many of you know or may have already heard, we have an unanticipated and unwanted passenger on board Siren of the Seas. It has been verified and confirmed the Southampton Strangler, a serial killer, is on board our ship."

There were murmurs among the crowd, and then it grew quiet. "As a member of our security team, you are well aware of how seriously Majestic Cruise Lines and Siren of the Seas takes security. As such, we are all on high alert until we can apprehend and secure the suspect."

A security guard raised his hand before speaking. "If you know who it is, why don't you arrest them and hold them until we reach Bermuda?"

"The evidence we currently have is circumstantial. Until the proper authorities can confirm such, we have nothing to hold the person in question."

Another guard chimed in. "You're not a hundred percent?"

"We're ninety-nine-point nine percent certain. The person in question will be under 24-hour surveillance, no exceptions," Patterson said. "We must remain vigilant, must remain on guard, and if you're wondering why I'm not releasing this individual's name and cabin number, it's because we need that last percentage."

And, Millie secretly suspected, *Patterson didn't want a gung ho guard attempting to single-handedly take down the suspect and risk having the entire case blow up in their faces.*

A few more questions were asked, and Nic and Patterson took turns answering before the meeting ended with a final reminder to remain vigilant.

Millie, along with Suharto, waited off to the side until the room cleared. They approached the front where the officers stood talking. She waited until they stopped and she caught Patterson's eye. "Well? Was I right?"

"As I told the others, we believe so. But as I mentioned earlier, there's a twist."

Chapter 23

"What's the twist?"

"Clarissa Sinclair injured the strangler by scratching them. At least, that's what the authorities surmised. Unfortunately, the tissue found under her fingernails doesn't belong to the suspect. They are working 'round the clock and hope to have a match soon."

"But for now, there's no smoking gun." Millie sucked in a breath. "If there's no smoking gun, there's no arrest."

"Correct."

"I have a plan. The strangler is after me. He believes I know too much."

"Which you do," Nic interrupted.

"The ironic part is he believed I knew too much before I even had a clue. I want to be the dangling carrot, to put myself in a position where he sees an opportunity to get rid of the one person he still views as a threat."

"How do you propose to do that?" Donovan asked.

"I'll need a little help." Millie outlined her tentative plan.

"I don't like it," Nic said. "This killer has eluded the authorities for years. He's clever."

"So are we," Millie insisted. "Our second option is for Suharto and me to wait for him to make his move, and I believe he will. Suharto can't follow me into every place—every public restroom, every nook and cranny."

Patterson began pacing. "Unfortunately, Millie is right. The walls are closing in. He may make a desperate move. Perhaps it's best if we play offensive instead of continuing on the defense."

Nic locked eyes with his wife, and for the first time, she saw fear. It mirrored her own. If they didn't act, there was no doubt in Millie's mind that she was "next."

"All right," Nic relented. "We can come up with a plan to pressure the killer into acting. For the record, I don't get a good feeling about this."

Each of them threw out ideas on how they could force the killer's hand. After everyone shared their thoughts, Millie repeated hers.

"Millie's idea makes the most sense," Patterson said. "We can strategically mobilize. There will only be a small window of time where she's vulnerable and facing the killer on her own...seconds, actually."

"The sooner, the better." Millie tapped Patterson's shoulder. "I have one request. I want to borrow your Viper."

"You could hurt yourself." He began shaking his head. "It's tricky and could easily backfire on you if you're not careful."

"I'm willing to take that chance."

Patterson stared at her for a long moment. "Fine. Daylight is burning. Let's put this plan into action."

*****

Suharto parted ways with Millie at the end of the hall. Despite all of her bravado, by the time she reached the Moxey's suite, she was sweating profusely, and her underarms were soaked. She wiped her clammy palms on her slacks before giving the door a light rap.

Kate Moxey answered. A puzzled expression flitted across her face when she saw Millie standing in the doorway. "Hello, Millie."

"Hello, Kate. I'm...I wondered if I might ask you a couple questions about...Hilda."

"Yes. Of course. Please come in."

Millie followed her inside. Harry was there, along with Annabel and Edward Ponsford. "I'm sorry to bother you again. I just...Hilda had sent me a photo she captured of a person she believed was following her prior to her death, and I can't help but believe it's a clue."

The Moxeys exchanged a quick glance. "Hilda photographed someone she thought was following her and sent it to you?" Harry asked.

"She did. I guess she didn't mention it?"

"No." Both couples shook their heads.

"Do you still have it?" Edward asked.

"I do." Millie pulled her cell phone from her pocket and clicked on the photo before passing it to Kate, who then handed it to Harry. "I've also shown a copy to our head of security. I'm not sure he put much stock in it since Hilda..." Millie's voice trailed off.

"Had a somewhat vivid imagination." Annabel finished her sentence.

"Right. I mean, I know he's taking the incident seriously." Millie glanced around and then lowered her voice. "Hilda thought she knew who it was."

"Did she give you a name?" Edward handed Millie her phone.

"No, but I got the impression she was talking about Bruce." Millie clasped her hands. "That's why I'm here—to find out if she confided in any of you."

"Regretfully, no," Harry answered. "The ship's head of security has questioned each of us at length. Hilda never mentioned anything of the sort."

"Have you shared your suspicions with Patterson?" Millie could've hugged Edward Ponsford for asking the question she wanted— needed—asked.

"Not yet. I already feel terrible about the tragedy. Heaping more distress on a grieving husband is the last thing I want to do."

"I don't believe it," Harry Moxey blustered. "I've known Hilda and Bruce for many years. Bruce is a devoted husband. He certainly isn't a serial killer."

"You know him better than I do. I'm not sure if I'll name names to Mr. Patterson yet. I want to give it some thought." Millie consulted her watch. "It's getting late. I need to head to my next event."

She exited the suite and strode to the end of the corridor, where she paused to collect her thoughts. Had she been convincing enough that the Ponsford's and Moxey's loyalty to their close friend would trigger them to tell him what Millie had said? Would it be a strong enough incentive for Bruce Ellis to come after Millie and try to take her out?

Millie reached into her pocket and ran her hand along the cold metal of Patterson's Viper. It was as close to a handgun as she could get. Now, the only question was...would she need to use it?

Chapter 24

Although Millie couldn't see them, she was certain Suharto and a good number of the ship's security department were lurking in the shadows, watching her from a distance.

She moved from event to event, mentally preparing herself for the moment when Bruce Ellis, the Southampton Strangler, popped out of the shadows and pounced on her.

The waiting was almost unbearable and, as the evening wore on, paranoia set in. Would he make a move? Perhaps he knew security was shadowing her and decided not to risk it. Or perhaps she had it all wrong. After all, the DNA under Clarissa's fingernails didn't belong to Bruce Ellis.

What if it was someone else—someone else in the group? But who?

Millie grabbed a quick bite to eat and then hosted a round of Killer Karaoke, followed by Blue Light bingo, a late-night bingo extravaganza. Her last stop was checking in at the Tahitian Nights Dance Club.

Still, nothing happened. No killer pounced on her from around the corner. When she reached the bridge, Suharto emerged from the shadows and joined her. "I did not see anyone following you."

"Neither did I." Millie slid her keycard into the slot and held the door for Suharto before they stepped onto the bridge. "Maybe I'm off. Maybe I had it all wrong, and Bruce isn't the killer."

"We are all wrong sometimes."

Nic, who was standing at the center console, hurried over. "Nothing?"

"Nope. Not a peep. I was so certain." Millie rubbed her brow. "How could I be so far off? The clues are all there."

"It's possible he noticed security tailing you and changed his mind."

"Tomorrow is a new day. Unfortunately, from everything I know about the strangler, he likes to strike at night."

By the time Millie and Suharto made up his sofa bed and let Scout out, Nic arrived home. The men stood talking in the kitchen while Millie excused herself. She trudged up the stairs and made quick work of getting ready for bed.

She and Scout had already settled in by the time Nic joined them. "I'm sorry this is dragging out."

"Believe me, no one wants this over more than me. I didn't have an inkling of being followed, even by the security detail. Maybe I'm losing my touch." Millie patted the blankets, waiting for Scout to take his spot in the center of the bed. "Or maybe I'm way off base."

Nic kissed her forehead. "I know you want to help Patterson and his men take this person down, but these things rarely go as planned."

"True," Millie murmured.

By the time Nic emerged from the bathroom, Millie, exhausted from being in fight-or-flight mode for hours on end, was already dozing off. She and Nic said their prayers, and the last thing she remembered before sleep took over was that Kate Moxey had remained almost silent during Millie's chat with her and the others.

Strangely quiet.

*****

Buzz. Buzz. Buzz.

Millie groggily swatted at her alarm clock, a low groan escaping her lips as she shut it off and rolled over. It took a few seconds for her to realize Nic's side of the bed was empty.

She flung the covers back and climbed out. Millie flew through her morning routine in record time and arrived downstairs to find Suharto and Nic savoring an early morning cup of coffee on the balcony.

"Good morning, dear," Nic said. "I have some wonderful news."

"About the strangler."

"Yes. Kate Moxey's been arrested." Nic told her the authorities matched the tissue found under Clarissa Sinclair's fingernails to Kate Moxey.

"Kate." Millie blinked rapidly, remembering how Kate had remained silent during her conversation with her, her husband, and the Ponsfords the previous evening. "How...why..."

"We don't know all the details yet. She's being held downstairs until we reach Bermuda where she'll be flown back to the UK."

"Has she confessed?"

"No. In fact, she's insisting she's innocent."

"Wow. All along, I thought it was Bruce Ellis."

Nic's cell phone chimed. "I need to head out. Patterson is holding a meeting to update the security department."

Suharto started to follow, and Nic stopped him. "As a precaution, I would like you to stay with Millie until we reach Bermuda and Kate Moxey is removed from the ship."

"Of course. I will be glad to."

"You're a good man." Nic squeezed Suharto's shoulder. "I also plan to meet with Patterson soon to discuss promoting you to level three security."

Suharto blinked rapidly as he puffed out his chest. "I will take a new position with pride."

"I'll see what I can do." Nic excused himself while Millie joined Suharto for her first cup of coffee.

There was a hint of humidity in the early morning air, and Millie could've sworn she heard the palm trees swaying, calling her name. They were almost home, and it made her heart happy.

While they enjoyed their free moments, Millie and Suharto discussed the day's schedule.

"You still look troubled, Miss Millie." Suharto studied her face.

"I'm not getting a warm and fuzzy. Something doesn't feel right." Millie checked her watch. It was late morning in the UK. "Halbert swears he saw the strangler on more than one occasion. I'm going to call him."

She dialed his number, and he picked up right away. "Hello, Millie."

"Hello, Halbert. How are you doing today?"

"Very well. A dockhand gave me his old fishing rod and tackle. I'm going fishing."

"That sounds like fun." Millie shifted the phone to her other ear. "The strangler has been caught."

"He has?"

"She. It's a woman. Her name is Kate Moxey."

"A woman?" Halbert grew silent. "They're wrong. It's a man. The strangler is a man. I would put my life on it."

"You're sure?"

"I am."

They chatted for a few more minutes. Millie thanked Halbert, promising to talk again soon, before ending the call. She waved the phone in the air. "Halbert swears the strangler is a man."

"We will talk to Patterson after his meeting. In the meantime, I will be with you, Millie. You will be safe."

"Thanks, Suharto." Millie exited the bridge, while Suharto hung back, planning to follow her from a distance.

Up first was Andy's before-the-crack-of-dawn, early morning staff meeting. She headed to the stairwell and began making her descent, mentally ticking off the list of things she needed to discuss with him. She wondered if Patterson had cancelled her guest services desk duty and then wondered if he would leave her probation in place since her hunch had proven to be wrong.

At least she had tried.

Millie covered the sets of stairs at a quick pace. She was almost to the employee exit, adjacent to the deck four passenger corridor, when she heard a *tink*.

She spun around, catching a glimpse of someone behind the cutout near the fire extinguisher.

With shocking speed, the shadowy figure was on top of Millie, dragging her to a nearby exit, a crewmember shortcut to a lower deck.

She tried to scream, but there was an unbearable pressure pressing down on her windpipe. Millie fought against the pressure and pain as she pried the Viper from her jacket pocket.

Her attacker had Millie's neck in the crook of his arm as he kicked the door open. In that moment, she realized if her attacker reached the railing, he could easily throw her over the side of the ship and into the ocean. No one—not security, not Suharto, would ever know what had happened to her.

She dug in her heels, blindly fighting back, kicking at the person who held her in a powerful grip. She began to feel lightheaded. With a burst of pure adrenaline, Millie shoved the Viper against her attacker's arm and pulled the trigger.

ZAP.

A jolt of pure electricity transferred from the Viper and through the strangler's long-sleeved jacket. In an instant, his death grip loosened, and Millie's attacker fell to his knees.

Bruce Ellis's cold-blooded black eyes—the eyes of a ruthless killer—stared back at her.

"Help!" The pressure on her windpipe made the cry for help little more than a desperate whisper.

She scrambled backward, her eyes never leaving Ellis.

As if possessed by some superhuman power, Bruce Ellis lunged forward and grabbed Millie's ankle. She fell hard on the concrete floor and began clawing her way to the stairwell.

Ellis's grip tightened and Millie screamed, this time louder.

A door banged shut.

"Millie!" Suharto's voice echoed in the stairwell.

"Down here," she wheezed.

Suharto bolted down the steps and flung himself at Millie's attacker.

As soon as Ellis released his hold on her ankle, she twisted sideways and went after him, zapping him a second time with the powerful stun gun. He jerked back, his body stiffening as he let out a garbled breath.

Suharto grabbed his radio. "Charlie! Charlie! Charlie! Aft stairwell deck four."

Things moved fast as security arrived on scene. Patterson was only seconds behind them.

Millie crawled to the wall and propped herself against it as she watched the security team pat Bruce Ellis down.

Patterson waited until his men cuffed the killer before joining Millie. "Are you okay?"

"I'm...I'm fine." Millie struggled to maintain her composure as the realization she'd almost died hit her full force. "He was choking me. He tried to drag me outside, to the railing." Her voice cracked. "He was going to throw me over the side. No one ever would've found me."

"You're safe now."

"Yes. Yes." The shock of what had almost occurred hit her full force, and a tear slid down her cheek. "Thank God we're all safe now."

*****

The head of security radioed Nic, who promised to meet them downstairs in Patterson's office. Suharto joined Millie, and they watched as he, along with a small army of security guards, escorted the handcuffed strangler down the steps and to the ship's holding cells.

They reached his office, and Millie's legs trembled as she sank into an empty chair near the door.

Nic burst into the room moments later and rushed to his wife's side. "Patterson said the strangler attacked you in the stairwell and tried to drag you outdoors."

"It was this close." Millie pinched her thumb and finger together. "He came out of nowhere. He was choking me and dragging me. Like I told Patterson, I would've vanished."

She pulled the Viper, the police grade stun gun, from her pocket and carefully placed it on his desk. "If not for this, I would've been dead. I've decided I'm going to put this on my Christmas list."

Chapter 25

It wasn't until the next day, after Millie had recovered from her near-death experience at the hands of the Southampton Strangler, that Sharky tracked her down and asked her to stop by.

He was in his office when Millie arrived, perched atop his PRV. Millie grinned when she spied Sharky's cat sprawled out in the basket attached to the front. "I see Finn is enjoying his new ride."

"We both are. I even upgraded to a larger basket to give him more room."

Millie scratched Finn's ears. He batted at her hand and began purring loudly as he playfully nibbled on her finger.

"I heard what happened yesterday morning. You're a celebrity around here and probably in

Southampton too," Sharky said. "I gotta say, you're pretty gutsy to take on the strangler."

"Not by choice. He was targeting me. Now that you mention it, there are a few blanks that need to be filled in. Do you mind if I give Patterson a call?"

"Be my guest."

Millie lifted her radio. "Patterson, do you copy?"

"Yes, Millie. Go ahead."

"I'm in Sharky's office and was wondering if you had any new updates."

"As a matter of fact, I just met with the captain and security staff. We're wrapping up our meeting. Hang tight, and I'll join you."

"10-4."

Sharky watched as Millie replaced her radio. "How did you..."

"Figure out who it was?" Millie pulled the now crumpled note from her pocket. "I knew I was on the strangler's radar, but I couldn't figure out why.

So, I started taking a closer look at his victims. Edith Branson was first. She and her husband were business owners. They owned a large manufacturing company in Southampton."

Millie handed Sharky the sheet. "The next victim was Sophie Young, a postgraduate student who worked alongside her father, a UK lawyer. The third victim was what triggered it for me. One of the stories I read mentioned she had been a recent juror, and not long after the trial, was convinced she was being stalked."

"Ah." Sharky ran his finger down the list. "Rich business owner, trial lawyer, juror."

"Bingo. Separately, it might not mean much, but then Nic and I were at a cocktail party that was attended by acquaintances of Clarissa Sinclair. One of them, Hilda Ellis, was convinced she was being followed and had snapped a blurry photo of her stalker. She showed it to me and then texted me a copy." Millie stopped, staring at Sharky expectantly.

"And…" Sharky rolled his hands. "You're the super sleuth. What am I missing?"

"Who would care about being photographed while stalking someone?" Millie answered her own question. "The Southampton Strangler, who was already suspected of being on board the ship."

"Okay, so the lady manages to snap a picture of some weirdo following her."

"Not just any weirdo. Her husband. My theory is Hilda suspected her husband, had known something was up. I think the last straw was during a conversation she and I had at that cocktail party. We were discussing the surveillance cameras on board the ship, how all the common areas are under surveillance. She told me she read stories of secret cameras being installed in hotel rooms and was going to check their cabin."

"And she found something else instead," Sharky said. "Something that implicated her husband."

"I believe so. That's why I told Patterson after Ellis tried taking me out to go back to Hilda and Bruce's cabin and tear it apart."

"To find what?"

Millie lifted a finger. "Good question, and one I hope he can answer."

"I heard Patterson arrested some chick after finding out she may have killed that reporter in Southampton," Sharky said.

"Kate Moxey. That's what I don't understand. How is Kate Moxey involved?"

There was a knock on the door. Patterson stepped inside, and he wasn't alone. Andy was with him. "There's our super sleuth hero."

"I have to admit, this one was a doozy," Millie said. "So, now that you have Bruce Ellis locked up and are getting ready to turn him over to the authorities in Bermuda, what did you find?"

"Remember when I mentioned a twist?" Patterson asked. "How the authorities discovered skin beneath Clarissa's fingernails, but determined it didn't belong to the strangler—Bruce Ellis?"

"Right."

"As you already know, it belonged to Kate Moxey. All the people in Clarissa Sinclair's party submitted DNA samples before boarding the ship. Hers was a perfect match."

"That's what I don't understand. Moxey was the strangler, too?"

"No. Bruce Ellis and Kate Moxey were having an affair. Clarissa must've somehow discovered it, she confronted Kate, they argued, and Kate killed her."

"Wait a minute." Millie did a timeout. "The Moxeys are swingers. Why would it matter?"

"Money." Patterson rubbed his thumb and fingers together. "According to the Ponsfords, Kate and Harry Moxey were moving to the US after being disinherited by their wealthy families because of their lifestyle. Kate was after Bruce Ellis's money. From what we can piece together, she planned to ditch Harry as soon as they reached the States."

"Because of the settlement," Millie guessed.

"We'll get to that. It all ties in together."

"Wow." Sharky let out a low whistle. "I guess it takes all kinds to make the world go 'round."

"Did you search the Ellis's cabin?"

"We did. We disassembled it piece by piece. There's a small cubby beneath the bathroom sink. It's used to access the pipes. We removed the panel and found some interesting items hidden there."

"A blue tennis shoe and a charm bracelet."

"Yes. Both items have been identified as belonging to the strangler's victims. Unfortunately, Hilda put your life in danger when she shared the picture of her stalker with you. All we can surmise is Bruce found the picture on her phone and noticed she'd forwarded a copy to you."

"Which, inadvertently, put me on the strangler's radar."

"It stands to reason."

Millie wagged a finger. "Now, there was another clue. After Hilda was found dead, I delivered flowers to the Ponsfords and Moxeys. They mentioned Hilda and Bruce's holiday home in Florida and then said something about some settlement money. That's when the lightbulb went off."

"Settlement money, manufacturing company, daughter, not to mention, employee of a trial lawyer, the juror," Patterson said. "The Ellises, after years of litigation, received a settlement from Edith Branson's company. The trial lawyer, Arthur Young, who represented Branson, managed to get the settlement amount reduced."

"Ah." Millie leaned her hip against the desk. "And the juror, the unidentified jogger, was in favor of the reduced settlement. Bruce was furious, so furious he decided to kill them. I've been trying to figure out how he ended up getting a substantial settlement until yesterday, when he tried to take me out."

"His eye," Patterson said. "Bruce Ellis lost one of his eyes in a warehouse accident while employed by Branson's manufacturing company."

"I wonder why he took a five-year hiatus and then started up again."

"I don't know." Patterson rocked back on his heels. "Maybe he figured the authorities were closing in and decided to cool it. There are some things in a serial killer's mind, or in any killer's mind, we'll never know. There's always a chance that Bruce Ellis wasn't the original strangler. It's something the authorities will have to figure out."

Millie reminded him of the incident when she suspected someone was following her in the stairwell. "It happened before Hilda forwarded the picture to me, and it threw me off."

"It could have been one of two things," Patterson said. "Number one, your overactive imagination was engaged."

"But Andy saw someone too," Millie insisted.

"I did," Andy said. "Although it could have been nothing and I could've avoided getting zapped."

"I am sorry for zapping you. I'm also sorry I ever suspected you of being the strangler."

"Me?" Andy's brows furrowed. "How could you possibly think it was me?"

"The fact that you left the ship early the same morning Clarissa's body was found and then, after discovering she'd managed to injure her attacker..."

Andy interrupted. "I came back with a shiner on my forehead."

"And scratches on your arm. By the way, how did you get the scratches?"

Sharky chuckled. "I can explain that. Better yet, I'll show you." He picked Finn up and carried him toward Andy.

The cat clung to Sharky, hissing loudly.

"Finn doesn't like you," Millie said.

"I never have done well with cats."

The cat recoiled, hissing a second time.

"See? I can't even get close to Finn." Andy stepped away from the hissing cat as he placed a hand over his chest. "Dogs, on the other hand, adore me."

"It could be your loud voice," Millie said. "Keep quiet and then try to pet Finn."

"He's going to attack me again."

"Andy," Millie chided.

"Fine," Andy whispered as he gingerly held out his hand.

Finn shrank back, and then his small black nose started to wiggle.

"Slowly."

With his hand palm up, Finn cautiously sniffed Andy before backing away.

"By George, I think you're onto something, Millie," he said in a soft voice.

She dusted her hands. "Another mystery solved."

"To answer the other part of Bruce's suspicions about you, my theory is he thought you and his wife were getting too cozy, and he was trying to scare you," Patterson said.

"Which makes the most sense. So, now it's time to toss out my probation and I have a credit for future use," Millie joked.

"Depending on what it is. I reserve the right to change my mind." Patterson turned his attention to Sharky. "Still enjoying your new set of wheels / rescue vehicle?"

"It's a sweet ride. I'm really looking forward to a nighttime water rescue practice run."

"We might be able to squeeze one in during our stopover in Bermuda."

Sharky's eyes lit. "I can't wait. Hey, Millie."

"No way. You'll have to find someone else for the next water rescue." Millie started shaking her head. "I've had enough excitement to last me for the rest of this voyage."

The end.

Dear reader, I hope you enjoyed reading "Southampton Strangler." Would you please take a moment to leave a review? It would mean so much. Thank you!

–Hope Callaghan

The Series Continues... Book 22 in Millie's Cruise Ship Mysteries -Coming Soon!

Annette's Healthy Greek Salad Recipe

Ingredients:

2- medium ripe red tomatoes, chopped

2-cucumbers, peeled and chopped

1 small red onion, chopped

½ head of iceberg lettuce, chopped

¼ cup olive oil

¼ cup Greek (Kalamata) olives, pitted and sliced

4 teaspoons lemon juice

2 teaspoons dried oregano

¾ cup crumbled feta cheese

Directions:

-In large bowl, mix tomatoes, cucumbers, red onion and iceberg lettuce.

-In small bowl, blend olive oil, olives, lemon juice, oregano and feta cheese.

-Pour oil mixture over salad mixture. Blend well.

-Chill in refrigerator before serving.

Meat Marinade Recipe

Ingredients:

1/4 cup olive oil

1/4 cup soy sauce

1-1/2 tablespoon lemon juice

1-1/2 tablespoons red wine vinegar

2-1/2 tablespoons Worcestershire sauce

1 tablespoon honey

2 teaspoons Dijon mustard

1 tablespoon minced garlic

1 teaspoon black pepper

Directions:

-Mix all ingredients.

-Marinade meat in refrigerator for 3-6 hours.

Annette's Tzatziki Recipe

Ingredients:

-One medium cucumber, peeled and quartered

-3 to 4 garlic cloves, finely minced

-3 tablespoons fresh dill, chopped

-1 teaspoon lemon zest (Optional. If you like tart, you can add more.)

-1 tablespoon extra-virgin olive oil

-2 cups Greek yogurt

-Salt and pepper to taste

-Pita chips, soft pita bread or cut vegetables

Directions:

-Grate peeled and quartered cucumber (I used a hand grater, but you can also use a food processor.)

-Place grated cucumber in small strainer over bowl to drain liquid.

-While cucumber is draining, place minced garlic, fresh dill, lemon zest and olive oil in medium size (sealable) bowl. Blend thoroughly.

-Add two cups yogurt. Blend.

-Place grated cucumber on a cheesecloth or double layer paper napkins and squeeze excess liquid out.

-Add cucumber to bowl. Stir thoroughly.

-Salt and pepper to taste.

-Cover tightly and refrigerate 3-4 hours.

-When ready to serve, stir thoroughly.

-Serve with vegetables, pita chips or wedges.

Read More by Hope

Cruise Ship Cozy Mystery Series

Hoping for a fresh start after her recent divorce, sixty something Millie Sanders, lands her dream job as the assistant cruise director onboard the "Siren of the Seas." Too bad no one told her murder is on the itinerary.

Made in Savannah Cozy Mystery Series

A mother and daughter try to escape their family's NY mob ties by making a fresh start in Savannah, GA but they soon realize you can run but you can't hide from the past.

Divine Cozy Mystery Series

After relocating to the tiny town of Divine, Kansas, strange and mysterious things begin to happen to businesswoman, Jo Pepperdine and those around her.

Garden Girls Cozy Mystery Series

A lonely widow finds new purpose for her life when she and her senior friends help solve a murder in their small Midwestern town.

Samantha Rite Mystery Series

Heartbroken after her recent divorce, a single mother is persuaded to book a cruise and soon finds herself caught in the middle of a deadly adventure. Will she make it out alive?

Sweet Southern Sleuths Short Stories

Twin sisters with completely opposite personalities become amateur sleuths when a dead body is discovered in their recently inherited home in Misery, Mississippi.

Meet Hope Callaghan

Hope Callaghan is an American mystery author who loves to write clean fiction, especially Christian cozy mysteries. She is the author of more than 70 mystery novels in six different series.

Born and raised in a small town in West Michigan, she now lives in Florida with her husband. She is the proud mother of 3 wonderful children.

When she's not doing the thing she loves best - writing books - she enjoys cooking, traveling and reading books.

Subscribe to her cozy newsletter for a free mystery ebook, new releases, and giveaways:
hopecallaghan.com

Made in the USA
Columbia, SC
25 June 2025

59832707R00231